Hammer Nail Foot

Little Book of Pain #1

Craig Brownlie

KOJ BOOKS

Please note that trigger warnings are at the back of the book.

***

Contents

LIFE IS A ROUGH DRAFT

Life is a rough draft

Without footnotes

Or time for

Adequate research

Forgive the misspellings

And obvious inanities

Trust the question mark

For it has your back

Condemn the

Run-on sentence

That lays waste the paragraph

Forgetting where it began

While losing sight of

The end

Under Construction

After Chris grew used to the pain in his foot, accepted his new sneakers were ruined, and realized no one looked for him, he remained unprepared for the humiliation of peeing his pants. Even so, he could look at the nail that secured his foot to the floor.

The pitter-patter of the rain on the roof had worked its magic. Chris tried to stand and unzip his pants, but his foot only hurt worse. Before a better idea presented itself, he felt the warm moisture creep across his crotch. He leaned forward as best he could, willing the liquid down his pants legs. A few drops leaked off the cuffs, but mostly he soaked his backside. Right away, the denim of his Kmart jeans turned frigid. Then they cracked as he shifted his weight back onto his butt. The chafing dug in next, worse than corduroys that time he fell while ice-skating.

***

Earlier, Chris felt things take a turn when they found the hammer. Whenever the gang explored one of the new houses going up in the neighborhood, they discovered all kinds of cool stuff. They never stole anything. Trespassing offered enough of a thrill. Add in a little wreckage and you beat the woods or the playground hands down.

Nails dotted the floor, as though one of the workers had spilled a bag. They bit through the soles of Keds like prickle bushes through a t-shirt. Karen found the bag beside the stairs and tossed handfuls at Stacy. Karen used to be the only girl to tag along with the boys so now she resented Stacy.

Chris resented both girls, but he wanted Eddie's approval more than anything. He accepted Eddie had no choice. Eddie had not been able to turn down Stacy after she punched him in the stomach.

Karen accompanied them because Eddie had killed her brother the summer before last. Chris had been there when Eddie and Darren had been playing catch with a knife. *The Magnificent Seven* showed on TV the night before and they needed to practice in case someone called on them to save a town of Mexicans. Everyone at the funeral whispered how Darren missed when the knife came to him. Chris knew Darren did catch the knife, though in the worst possible way.

Chris pissed Eddie off all afternoon. First, he wanted to ride bikes without stopping by the construction site. Then, he would not go inside until Eddie called him a "chicken" like five times. The real deal breaker came when he refused to pee into the basement when the other boys did. Chris knew he had been asking for it.

Eddie found the hammer in the woodpile outside. Usually the first one to tromp around in the mud, he laid claim to anything outside. His best discovery had to be the windows under the tarp in the backyard. They lay out of sight of the street with only the woods behind them.

The gang lined up a row of windows against the base of the house, breaking only one pane when the hammer slipped. Eddie refused to put it down even when carrying stuff.

Everyone helped make an ammo pile of stones. Eddie took the honor of the first throw, breaking glass. Karen had the best arm in the group, so she threw next. They worked their way through everyone. On Eddie's second turn, he handed the hammer to Chris. Chris liked the heft of it and held on to it a little too long until Eddie wrenched it out of his hand.

Chris carefully selected a stone which felt a good weight. He had a good eye and usually hit the hat when flinging baseball cards. He leaned back and put all he had into it. The stone landed on the mark, but bounced off, breaking nothing.

"It hit the frame." He looked at Eddie, "You hurt my wrist."

"No, you missed," declared Eddie. "You've always been lame."

Chris responded by mumbling he was not lame so Eddie would not hear. "At least, I don't throw so hard it's impossible to catch." He was glad Eddie ignored him.

Bored with the game, Eddie grabbed a 1x6 and made a ramp to the rear door of the house. Chris followed everyone back inside, though Eddie made it as difficult as possible by shaking the board when Chris reached halfway up.

They explored the upstairs last because the carpenters had not put in the landing's floorboards. Stacy showed how you must be a wuss if you would not walk along the edge of the landing to the next set of stairs, so the whole gang followed. Eddie ensured no one stayed behind by bringing up the rear. Chris knew better than to argue. The sun went to twilight, so they had no time to waste before dinner. Good enough at balancing, Chris made it, no problem.

On the second floor, they scattered among the rooms, tugging on exposed wiring, and sliding random junk into the open walls. Car headlights shown through the house skeleton.

"Someone's here!" echoed through the house. Almost everyone assumed Chris had called out, though Chris knew he had not. People scooted to street-side and peered out. Soon, the all-clear sounded. Eddie berated Chris for being such a freakin' wimp. Then Eddie let loose a string of curse words to prove he knew how in case anyone thought otherwise.

Various voices announced they needed to head home before it became any darker. The rain started, too. Their bikes were going to sink deep in the mud back in the woods if they didn't drag them free soon.

Heading down the stairs and across the landing, they repeated their original order. Chris took a few steps and stopped. The opening looked much bigger from above.

Chris and Eddie remained, staring at one another like Sheriff Matt Dillon facing down some bad hombre for the final gunfight. When he understood Chris had been struck immobile, Eddie said, "You have to be fucking kidding me."

Karen picked up a couple nails off the floor and threw them up at Chris. Then the others joined in. Stacy yelled at them to stop when the nails fell back on their own heads.

Suddenly, Eddie charged at Chris and knocked him over, "Fine, stay if you wanna stay!"

Stunned Chris fought back the first tears. Landing on a nail hurt more than the betrayal. Friends sometimes acted up.

"What? You're going to cry now?" demanded Eddie.

Chris shook his head.

Eddie grabbed something off the floor. "You're a crybaby, aren't you?" Eddie held a nail in one hand and the hammer in the other.

"What are you going to do, Eddie? Kill me like you did Darren? You threw that knife too hard." Chris tried to claw the words back into his mouth.

Then Eddie placed the nail over Chris' foot and pounded.

Chris screamed in pain.

"Shut up! Shut up! Shut up!" yelled Eddie, rising to his feet and clutching the hammer in a fist held high.

Everybody downstairs demanded to know what had happened. After Eddie said nothing and Chris whimpered, Stacy climbed to the landing. When she saw, she covered her mouth to keep in the scream. Leaning over the stairs, she announced, "Eddie nailed Chris' foot to the floor!"

Downstairs emptied as everyone ran for their bikes.

Dropping the hammer, Eddie headed to ground level. Stacy called him back. "You want to help him, help him," said Eddie.

Chris looked awfully pale. Stacy picked up the hammer like she wanted to help Chris, but she could not approach his messed up foot. Then Chris passed out.

After waking up and before wetting his pants, Chris tried to figure out what to do. He whispered for Eddie and Stacy and a litany of other names. He called loudly for Eddie once, but the outburst made his foot hurt more.

For the first time, he took a good look at the nail sticking out of the top of his sneaker. He couldn't tell if anger or nausea clouded his vision. He tried out the F-word and it felt good in his mouth.

Eddie had done a fine job hammering the nail into the floor. It looked to be one of the big ones used to stick 2x4's together. Blood leaked from the bottom of the shoe, but only a little coated the top. His foot hurt, though not as much if he held still. He could deal with the pain when he sat back and kept his foot flat.

He tugged on the nail which made his leg wobble. He almost passed out again. He thought about ripping his foot free, but his strength could not budge the sneaker sole. Chris felt queasy the more he thought about it.

How long could it be before someone came looking? His dad must be home from work by now. They wouldn't eat dinner without looking for him.

"Help!" called Chris, but his throat hurt after one outcry. He hadn't recognized his growing thirst. The thought made him want to pee and that was that.

His tears tasted good while he thought about someone finding him covered in piss. He wiped his leaking eyes and adjusted to the dark. The moon must have peeked through the clouds in the last few minutes because Chris could see the hammer handle sticking out above the top step of the stairs.

If he turned away from it, then he might be able to lean back and reach the hammer. The first time he tried to pivot on the nail, he tasted acid from his stomach. Something in his shoe came loose with a push and a twist. He made it the rest of the way by gritting his teeth. He swallowed some vomit after it erupted into his mouth.

Sliding his butt forward and bending his knees way up, Chris leaned back onto the floor and reached as far out as possible. The top of the stairs proved closer than expected. He fought the feeling of falling backwards. Stretching his arm, he grabbed the hammer and swung it forward, doing a sit-up. He felt dizzy with the effort.

Next, he had to find purchase for the hammer claw. The nail sat low enough in the shoe, so the hammer needed to leverage on part of his foot. The first tug made him pass out again.

Chris woke to the sound of padded feet downstairs. He recognized Tommy's dog, Shep. Maybe Chris could tie a note or something to it's collar, "Here, boy!" His throat felt full of the sawdust which covered the floor. Chris coughed and called until the dog looked up with a goofy question on its face. Shep charged the steps, only to stop in a skid at the open landing. Then he backed down two, ran at the opening with all his might, and leapt across.

Chris contorted to offer an embrace to Shep. Instead, the German shepherd circled around to face him from a few feet away.

"Good boy," muttered Chris.

Shep licked his lips and let out a soft growl.

"You smell the blood don't you, boy," said Chris. "Well, it's only my foot." Chris pointed at the mess at the bottom of his leg.

Shep accepted the invitation and went to bite the foot. Chris howled and swung the hammer, hitting the dog in the center of the head, driving Shep's teeth deeper into the sneaker. Chris screeched in pain. Shep made a sound like air leaking out of a bike tire and lay very still.

Chris tapped the side of Shep's head with the hammer, but it only shifted the skull back and forth. He kept tapping until Shep's jaw moved away. His foot felt very cold as soon as the warm dog head uncovered his sneaker. Then, his lower leg went from numb to excruciating and back again. Afraid to pass out anymore, Chris jammed the hammer claw under the nail head and pulled with all his might. Chris heard an awful howl in the room, but he could not tell for certain where it came from.

Hanging onto the hammer, he crawled down the stairs to the gap of the unfinished landing. He tossed the hammer onto the first floor and considered dropping after it.

Discarding that thought, he moved his butt along the edge of the landing frame, an almost too narrow piece of wood. Sliding across the hole, his mangled foot dripped blood onto the flooring below.

Chris grabbed the hammer. By the time he left the house, he hopped okay with the aid of an extension pole left by the work crew. At the edge of the woods, he found his bike, alone against a tree. If he kept the injured limb out of the way, then he could pedal with one foot more easily than he expected.

Chris would tell his parents about the bike accident. They would fix him up and feed him. Before hopping inside, he hid the hammer in the garage. He would pick it up in the morning on his way to school. No one would notice it in his backpack until afterwards when he caught up with Eddie on the afternoon walk home.

THE COVENANT

And tomorrow they will take from you that first piece of flesh
But you wouldn't know that
Because you don't know anything

It could be preserved in tin foil and placed in the freezer
But no one would do that
Because no one does that sort of thing

Someday you could unwrap it with trembling fingers
But it would be blue and wrinkled
Because it is a piece of you

How I Came In Fifth In The 2022 Scares That Care Gross Out Contest

And walked away with five dollars from Brian Keene's wallet

I told this story:

Arthur C Clark! You may not know that he spent much of his life living on Sri Lanka. That island nation has been in the news because of the peaceful overthrow of their government recently.

But Arthur C Clark knew other tales of the country as he told me during a lunch break at a Massachusetts con a few decades ago. It began when he leaned over from an adjoining table and said, "I wouldn't eat that fish if I were you. I've given up on fish."

Art, if I may call him that, told me about recent deaths among his countrymen. Initially, it had been blamed on the Ceylon Kissing Fish, much like the Amazonian candiru which swims into people when they urinate in fresh water and lodges in the urethra.

Men have described the sensation of a little tickle on the end of the penis, giving the local catfish its name. Later, the red pus oozing from the end of the penis would be the first hint of problems to come.

Local remedies for removal were brutal because of the barbs along the tiny fish's body. Tiny sticks were inserted, and a hard tug usually led to unconsciousness.

With an aw shucks grin, Art called them Penile Piscine Probers. Still, the patient survived. Then people started dying before the Kissing Fish could be extracted.

The culprit was the South Indian Ocean Tapefish, which had benefited from overfishing of its natural predators. The Tapefish lays its eggs in other fish, notably their swim bladder and they had recently encroached on the Sri Lanka coast, where they preyed upon the local sturgeon.

Now, in Sri Lanka, an absolute treat is fish maws, made from the swim bladder of the local sturgeon. Tapefish roe will normally pass through a person like street cart fish maws through a tourist, unless something bad happens. As it turns out, the Ceylon Kissing Fish loves nothing better than Tapefish roe.

So, you stop for a quick lunch of fish maws and ingest Tapefish eggs.

The next day, you wade into the local lake to catch dinner. The Kissing Fish swims up your penis and digs its tiny barbs into the root.

The blood and pus start leaking out. You grunt for an hour, as bruising spreads in your groin. The Kissing Fish smells those baby Tapefish buried a couple inches away. You sense something horribly wrong as your intestines shift in your belly.

The Kissing Fish starts spinning side to side and drills an unnatural passage from the root of the penis through to the closest intestine and slowly crawls through that tiny tunnel, gobbling everything available.

You fart, raising a personal miasma of salt, iron, crap, and ocean rot. Your last sensation is brown, green mush leaking from your anus, a combination of blood, semen, urine, and fish shit.

And four people told better stories. Not a word of my story is true.

STRIP MINING BEAVERS

The strip mining beavers came to stay.
At least, that's what they constantly say
In the bar or on the street
To anyone that they meet.
The beavers arrived only yesterday

They made a big hole west of town
Causing the collapse of the playground.
Plus, the junior high
Has begun to slide
Past town hall and continues on down.

The streams are filled with run-off.
Most of the children have a cough.
The beavers don't care.
They'll do this everywhere.

Until the townsfolk have had enough.

To All NW.L.L. Families

To all Northwest Little League Families and Boosters!

Welcome back for another great year of baseball and fun! As many of you have expressed concerns to me over the past few months, let me say right up front that we do plan to put last year far behind us. Still, let's not forget the lessons learned! As they say, "objects in the mirror may be closer than they appear"! Bearing that in mind, let's review some news and changes for this, our glorious 47th season! (For those expressing concern that last year was also our 47th season, let me remind you that the paint used on the fences last spring was donated by Mundy Hardware. According to the EPA, we should be able to celebrate our 50th season back in Bloomington Park in three short years!)

-The retirement of Coach Kennedy means we're looking for a fresh face to manage our T-Ball team. As some of you know, Coach K's wife gave birth to twins during the final game of last season, giving the Kennedy's just enough to field a team of their own (and all under the age of eight!). Hurry back, Marc! We'll miss those wild-haired tantrums and red-eye practices!

-This year's opening Day ceremonies will feature Britney Spears and former President Bush! —Just kidding! Let's remember to laugh together all season long! Hard and often!

-Seriously, Sheriff's Deputy Malcolm "Dizzy" Cosgrove will be back to sing the national anthem, accompanied as always by his brother on accordion and his nephew on sousaphone. And Commissioner Bloomington may again have some "fireworks" in store if he can make it across the state border before the big day! Let's hope for the best and send your Independence Day orders to Lou by mid-March.

-Our umpires this year will be coming from South Barton. For those of you unfamiliar with South Barton, it is 60 minutes due south on the interstate in light traffic. Let's be sure to give these newcomers a traditional big Northwest welcome before every game. And keep in mind, we never double-park beside an umpire's car!

-Reminder to all parents and players: athletic protection is not just for catchers. Be sure to wear your cups to every practice and game. Also, attend our pre-season training session: Dodging Hard One-Hop Ground Balls Is A Moral Imperative. This session is required for all coaches and infielders by our new insurance carrier. In a related matter, our best wishes go out to Tamla Bindle on his continuing recovery. We understand the remaining wounds are only psychological. So, if you see Tamla on the street, give him a big Northwest Little

League pat on the back and tell him how much his voice has lowered.

-As usual, please review the revised list of words that should not be heard in the stands. This year, the entire list has been translated into Pig Latin due to the demonstrative efforts of Mrs. EnnedyKay and Mrs. LoomingtonBay. Our thanks go out to Kennedy Farm Products for providing the "Language Enforcers" to volunteers from Northwest Evangelical Lutheran Church who will be seated among our fans.

-As with the second half of last season, we'll be playing behind Northwest Middle School on the soccer fields. Because of our need to coordinate with summer soccer, there will be no Saturday practices or games. The volunteers from Northwest Evangelical Lutheran Church have requested rest on Sundays, so all games and practices will be scheduled on weekday evenings. Through mid-May, please park near the sidelines and train your headlights on the base paths. If possible, practice catching fly balls at home during the day. The soccer league has requested that we watch out for divots and avoid hanging from the soccer goals. That means you, parents! Ha, ha! Really.

-Realizing that your humble commissioner may be from a different generation, let's take this opportunity to remember that facial piercing and headfirst sliding do not mix, as we all learned from Dominic Kennedy last season. Once again, our gratitude goes out to Dr. Bindle for reattaching Dominic's eyebrow. Who else knew you could sterilize baseball stitching in Gatorade?

-The annual awards ceremony will be one week after the final game of the season. Golden Parent Awards will be given to every parent or guardian who attends every game. Since so many of you are using these in custody hearings, Family Court has informed us attendance can only be credited for sitting in the stands or on the sidelines. Beer drinking in the parking lot no longer counts.

-Last, but not least, the Middle School will be closed during summer evenings. The fast food restaurants along West Macon Avenue have requested our players and especially their parents be reminded to use the bathroom before leaving home for games.

Let's make this our best season ever! At least, let's make it our best 47th season yet!

BOILING WATER

I stood at the stove
Boiling water in a pot
The coffee hovered in a strainer
On the kitchen table
When she burst in
And said she wanted to help with the laundry
Specifically the sheets

We stuffed what we could
Into my broken bags
And hauled the loads to the laundromat
Where we sat through the cycle
Waiting to see how the stains would turn out
Especially the sheets

BUGS, NOSE, FAULKNER

Bugs on the keys again. It always starts this way. I hate the damn things, always crawling under my fingers, catching beneath the tips, squirting their guts out across my desktop blotter.

I love plastic. It's so smooth, not like bug guts which are slippery. They never give me a new keyboard when the old one is covered with bug slime.

I learned at my old job. I would call the help desk and they would send somebody over, but they stopped. My old boss told me to quit bothering the nice people at the help desk. I told him about the bug guts and then I had to find a new job.

Now, when the bugs come, I put the keyboard in the top drawer of my desk and sit back and stare out my window. When I open my drawer up again, the bugs are gone. I think they live in the back of the drawer, but I am too afraid to look.

The janitor cleans them out once a week, but he does not understand they come back every night.

I am going to call the help desk anyway, but I will not tell them what is wrong.

Everyone is all excited in Judy's cube. She overflowed with bugs and fish last night. I could tell by looking at her they had to be the long squirmy kind, like lampreys. I saw a picture of a lamprey once. It looked like a penis before the bugs come and bite off the tip.

Bugs, buggy, buggering Bugs Bunny. I love rabbits, George.

Old movies are great. I have watched a million of them. They used to show them every Friday night in the big hall where they fed us. I think they put bugs in the food and waited to see when they would crawl out of us. I closed my eyes when I ate because I felt afraid to look at the food.

The nice people at the help desk say they will send someone over to fix my keyboard. I told them the keys do not work.

Have you ever heard of John Steinbeck? He knew about the bugs, I could tell. Martha read to me from some words he wrote. I told her about the bugs before anyone.

Martha said some guy named Burroughs knew about the bugs, but I felt afraid when she tried to tell me about him. I saw his picture on the back of the book she held and he looked like a mean old man. But he knew about the bugs.

Martha has such soft hands. I remember her fingers curling around the edges of the book. Her thin, colored nails scampering along the sides of the pages. Sometimes her nails sprouted legs and popped off her hands and ran about on the carpet. She would scream at first, but later we would laugh and laugh.

I love Martha.

A spider swings from a thread outside my window. It looks like a needle on the end of a tube after you have taken it out of your arm even though they do not want you to.

Lampreys look a lot like worms. Worms squirm beneath the epidermis. I once ate a worm. It didn't taste anything like chicken like Jose said it would. I never talked to him again. He didn't know anything about bugs or worms or anything, anyway. He said he did, but he lied.

People who lie have bugs coming out of their mouths.

Have you ever seen the inside of a person?

Lies sound like bugs and worms crawling across your tongue. My mommy could make the bugs and worms go away. I miss her a lot sometimes.

Martha says everyone misses their mother sometimes, but you must get over it. Martha's very smart that way, don't you think? I do not think she knows about Judy, though. I never tell her about any of the others because I do not want to upset her. Sometimes she asks if there is anyone else, but I tell her no. Then I must run out of the room because of the bugs which will burst from my mouth any minute now.

I have a big window because I am important. I type all day whatever they tell me to type and they pay me, and I like my job. I have my own cubicle with cloth walls and a little desk.

I have two file drawers!

I watch the spider outside my window as he swings back and forth like he's on a trapeze.

I really, really like going to the circus. I once saw somebody fall from the trapeze. Her partner didn't catch her, and she fell and fell until she broke on the ground.

Something is crawling across my tongue. I can feel its little legs stepping so softly as its wings beat against the roof of my mouth. I hate when this happens.

If I try to cough it out, then it grabs hold tighter and tighter until my tongue turns purple. I can open my mouth and hope it leaves. I wish it would fly away, but it's crawling up my cheek out of my mouth. It's big, too big, and it looks like a praying mantis. I really hate when this happens.

I lied about the magnificent girl on the flying trapeze. She didn't die even though I thought she would. She fell in a net, but, really, she should have been dead. I think nets are like lying.

Bugs on the girl, bugs big as a cat, bugs on the girl because she didn't go splat.

William Faulkner is a funny man. Martha loved to read his stories. I buy his books whenever I see them at garage sales. I ask the owners why they're selling them, and they always say the same thing, "My daughter brought it home from college and left it when she got married."

Martha does not approve of co-eds. They do not like her too much either. They go to the little girls' room and make sick after they meet her.

Sometimes I try to write because I think Martha has read everything by William Faulkner and she might want to read something else. With bugs in it. Everything I write has bugs in it.

I hate the daughters who forget about William Faulkner. They think they're better than Martha and they're wrong. I know this because they say so. I meet them in clubs and in libraries and at work. I look for them, but I will never marry them because they're married already. It's what they tell me, anyway.

This job is easy if the bugs stay away. When they first appeared, I thought maybe it happened because I ate at my desk, so I always ate my lunch in the cafeteria. I never even sipped water at my desk, even when my lips cracked, and my eyes itched.

The bugs came anyway, and I gave up. I still do not eat at my desk, but I am watching my figure. I need to stay trim so Martha will always love me. A trim limb is a good limb. Martha likes my lamprey.

I remember staying in the house with many beds. Father said I had to go, and mommy did not love me enough to stop him.

I had a mean neighbor named Mr. Nose once, but he does not live next to me anymore. All my neighbors are nice now. I like them better that way. Rude people always tell you what they think when you ride with them on the elevator. They complain because they think you are making the building stink.

Mr. Nose even called the police, but they did not smell anything. I bought stuff you plug into the wall and stuff you pump and stuff you spray, and the cop said it smelled like a whorehouse, but they could do nothing about it. Nose knows nothing.

I went to the circus every night after the girl fell from the trapeze. She had thick, strong legs and never fell again. I felt a little disappointed, but she could not fall every night. She fell for me on my first night. I watched her hands wherever she held on as she swung. I loved her strong hands and thick legs. When the ringmaster announced the circus would leave town, I stayed after the show and talked to the girl.

We walked by the creek. She liked my nice, big hands. Hers were not as big as mine. I saw a lamprey in the creek, but she said it looked more like a crawdad. She liked movies, too, she said, but I think she lied. I do not know when she started lying, but bugs came out of her mouth. More and more, they raced out of her, but I could not help her.

Stream screams, we all scream for ice cream.

I followed Mr. Nose home from work one night because I wanted to know what he thought he smelled. Do not tilt your head back, a bloody Nose needs pinching. Streams of blood and bugs. Ice cream! With worms.

William Faulkner eats bugs!

Judy's parents sold me her copy of **Absalom, Absalom**. She had signed her name on the inside front cover, and I found her in the telephone book. A, B, C, easy as you please. D, E, F, how many more are left?

Judy has very nice parents, but I hear her talking with her mother all the time. She sounds like a little girl, even littler than the magnificent girl on the flying trapeze. Judy is married, but I do not care.

How do spiders rise so high? I am on the eighteenth floor. If he is swinging outside my window, then he must be coming down from somewhere. Do you think he climbed all the way to the top to swing all the way down to the bottom?

Sometimes I hug my window. I kneel on the ledge in front of it and spread out my arms as wide as I can. I press my cheek against the glass and breathe in and out. I can see down out of the corner of my eye.

I am not afraid to fall if the spider isn't. I leave a breath stain when my boss makes me pull away from the window. She always tells me it is not as hard as I might think to replace me, but I do not care. I can leave my job now.

I once ate a spider. What goes in must come out. Jose taught me to tear the legs off it first. The trick is not to taste it and swallow fast. Over the lips and past the gums, watch out stomach, here it comes. Without the legs.

The magnificent girl on the flying trapeze had thick legs. Martha has thin legs. Judy's legs are just right.

My monitor is a bug like I have never seen before. A hand is grabbing me. It feels like my father's hand. I type all day and stare at the monitor. The hand is telling me to type. Press the keys.

The spider has blown away to I know not where, which is where my father said I live -- I know not where. And I never went back. I wonder what the spider thinks of his thread. I wonder what the thread thinks of the spider. I wonder what I think. I wonder what I thread.

Ding, dong, the witch is dead.

The receptionist is passing out a notice about Judy, but I already know what it says. Judy will not be in to work today. She has a bug.

I never call in sick, but it is a point of pride with me. My father taught me right. You won't be on a team if you're not there when they're picking sides. Judy's parents are probably nice, but they did not teach her right.

Judy never saw a lamprey before, so I told her I had one.

I wonder what a lamprey eats. I should know, but I do not. I love books, but I never have time to read. I buy books for

Martha. She likes old books, dusty books, yellow books. The smelly ones do not bother her.

Judy stayed late last night. So did I.

I open the notice about Judy with my nose and hold it really close to my face. I like to read this way.

The police are here and want to talk to us. They might want to hear about the bugs. I hear them talking to her friends, but I try to ignore them.

The police always take the side of the rude people. Copper, flatfoot, pig.

My house smells better than your house. I better pick up more room deodorizer on my way home.

Judy did not want to meet Martha, but I knew she lied because I saw the bugs coming out of her face. First, a little grasshopper stuck its tiny head out of her nose and looked around. Then, a big old beetle crawled out of her ear and down her cheek. I slapped it to knock it off, but I only made her mad. I am supposed to count when I feel mad.

One, two, three, four, five, six, seven, eight, nine, ten. When I reach ten, I can do whatever I want.

Bugs, rugs, slugs. Girl twirls. Skin like paper in an old book. Blood like bugs. Spiders like needles. Love like death. Faulkner likes me.

I miss Judy already. Martha says it is only natural. Martha does not care though. She is glad Judy is gone. So is William Faulkner.

Here comes the man. Hear his footsteps. It's the nice man from the help desk to make the bugs go away. He says he passed the police on their way out. I wonder if my next job will be as nice. I went to a garage sale on Saturday and bought a copy of **The Sound and the Fury**.

The Age Of Clark Kent

What's the point in fighting crime?
We are
Not all superheroes
Even in our dreams

The age of Clark Kent
And Superman's descent
Bizarro speech
And tripping on the cape

Smallville is so far away
And Lois is the future
All Lois all the time

THE SMARTEST MAN ON THE FLOOR

David owed Marc for the thing he did for David last month, so he sent Marc two American Repertory Theatre opening night tickets for the same night he intended to attend, though in different sections.

David brought his current significant other and Marc brought his woman of the moment. David knew Marc since they had tagged blue line MBTA cars in high school.

The two couples connected in the lobby during the intermission. Marc reintroduced David to Daphne. They had met once before, but formality dictated at the theatre. Marc's date proved pleasant enough. She had the disinterested look Marc sought in a short-term relationship. David licked his lips while he shook her hand.

"And this is Bella," David said, gesturing to a graceful woman approaching their trio and bearing a drink from the bar. To Marc's eyes, Bella floated toward them on a half shell. Marc had never met his friend's bride-to-be. Her long, dark hair swung to and fro, framing the subtle fluctuations beneath her skin-tight, scarlet dress. The few silver hairs within her mane twinkled like mineral deposits demanding excavation. Her eyes simmered through the purest black of the bottomless depths of the deepest trench in the unexplored oceans.

And then she spoke.

"You must be Marc," she mouthed, but he heard an exquisite, sensual melody.

Dumbfounded until Daphne elbowed him, Marc recovered slowly and introduced Daphne to Bella.

"How do you like the show?" David asked, disinterestedly.

Daphne replied, "It's kind of slow, isn't it. I fell asleep about half way into it."

"A lot of people have trouble with the theatre," said David, putting his hand on Daphne's arm.

"I always enjoy Strindberg," said Bella. "I find him energizing. The ideas fly about on the stage. What do you think, Marcus?"

"I really like the actress..." He struggled to concentrate on the question, let alone remember the play.

Bella continued. "The way Auguste captures the tension created by the bourgeois mentality pressing down upon the less empowered sections of his era's populace, while pushing the upper strata of society to their wits' end and then using this to reflect the struggle between the genders demonstrates where his concerns centered and reinforces the contention they had arrived at a turning point in society's procession."

The other three nodded in agreement.

"Those wacky Scandinavians," Marc concluded.

Everyone smiled politely and stood in place studying one other, the ground, their hands, and then each other again. Marc stared mostly at Bella.

David said he had to hit the men's room. Marc followed. They did a little coke.

The lights flashed for the end of intermission and the two couples said their farewells. Bella shook Marc's hand. When he pulled his hand away, a business card rested in his palm. He shoved the card in his pocket without looking and took Daphne by the arm.

While Daphne slept through the second half of the play, Marc pulled out the card and read: "Bella van der Paris. H: 555-BELLa. Call Me." He shoved the card back into his pocket.

Daphne dozed on the shoulder of the elderly woman sitting on her far side. He thought about Bella until the play concluded. Then he thought about Daphne again. She did have ways of making him concentrate his attention solely on her.

Marc's job usually distracted him, but, by the next afternoon, he had fully recovered from Daphne and refocused on Bella. He pulled out her card and dialed the number. An answering machine picked up: "Greetings, this is Bella and I can't come to the phone right now but be sure to leave your name and number. I'll get back to you first thing." He hung up without leaving a message, hating answering machines.

Marc called David at work. David's secretary told him his friend had called in sick. Marc asked the secretary if she might be free for dinner. She declared herself a married woman. He asked her if she'd be free next week then. She hung up as she usually did.

Marc called David at home, reaching another answering machine. After Rod Stewart quit crooning into his ear, Marc said. "This is Marc. How's it hanging? Did Bella wear you out?" He heard a click on the end.

"This is David. What's up, Marc?" David sounded tired.

"I wanted to grab beers with you. Find out about this Bella."

"Nothing much to find out." David sounded ready to fall asleep.

"You sound wicked wrecked," Marc tried.

David said, "I must be coming down with something."

"You spent the night alone?" doubted Marc.

"She gave me a hell of a hickey," David's voice sounded hoarse. "I didn't go for it and she left. She probably gave me mono. How'd things go with Daphne?"

"The usual," Marc replied.

"So, you're okay today?" David acknowledged.

"A little tired, but not sick like you," Marc answered. "You mind if I call Bella?"

David paused a second. "You mind if I call Daphne?"

"It's a free country," Marc said, already deciding he would.

"All right then," said David.

"Okay."

"Goodbye."

"Goodbye." Marc hung up and sat at his desk, staring at the phone.

Marc went to the tavern by his office after the gym. He sat outside and drank, watching the sun go down, painting the sky a brilliant red.

After a few minutes, he went inside and used the payphone to try Bella again. She answered. "Hi, this is Marc," he told her.

"Marc?" She had trouble placing the name.

"Marcus from the play last night," he reminded her.

"Yes," Bella said.

Marc heard her smile.

"You'll have to forgive me. I just woke up."

This had indefinable appeal. "Oh?"

"I... took a nap when I arrived home from work." Bella sounded confused.

"Listen," Marc said, "I'm sitting here outside of Louie's Tap enjoying a good drink on a cool night. What do you say to joining me?"

"I shouldn't." Bella paused.

Marc assumed she was thinking it over.

Bella sighed. "I'll be there in twenty minutes."

"You know where Louie's is at?"

"I'll find you," Bella hung up.

Marc held the phone marveling at how well he had handled his approach, hoping the landing would go as smoothly. He would be impressed if she actually arrived in twenty minutes. The nearest decent apartment had to be at least fifteen minutes away by cab.

Closer to forty-five minutes, Bella wore a wrap around her waist which fluttered to the rhythm of Marc's heartbeat. Moonlight followed her path and danced about her silhouette. "Good evening, Marcus," she said to him.

"You look ravishing," Marc smiled at her.

She sat. They ordered drinks. He had a martini and she had a Bloody Mary. The conversation seemed brilliant and divine. "What do you do?" He asked after the drinks arrived.

"I'm a nurse," she said.

"Which hospital?" asked Marc.

"For the Red Cross, actually."

"Sounds like interesting work."

Bella knew a great deal about blood. Marc listened while she described drawing blood from a donor, but he did not hear her words. He enjoyed the perfume she wore.

After they drained the second round of drinks, Bella invited him back to her place.

Fate could be truly kind to those she found appealing. Marc hailed a cab, but Bella told him not to bother. She lived within walking distance. They strolled arm in arm the few blocks into the heart of the warehouse district. She had owned a loft for many years.

They rode a freight elevator to the top floor of a two story structure. Pitch black until she turned on the lights, the bulbs buzzed overhead bathing the wide-open space in an eerie glow. Worn furniture from a variety of periods gave the place a well-used, comfortable feel. Shadows danced on the distant walls as the lights flickered overhead.

Bella told him the warehouse had once been on the docks before developers had built out over the water, adding landfill as they went. If you tried hard, you could still smell the sea in the timbers which made up the building. Marc sniffed at a nearby wall, but only noticed a termite navigating the paneling.

Bella led him by the hand to a sofa. He sat and she offered him another drink. He asked for a beer. She offered a Bloody Maria, saying she had them mixed in the refrigerator. He said anything would be fine with him.

She went to the kitchen.

Marc passed out. He could only handle seven beers and two martinis.

When Marc came around, he lay on the sofa, covered with a blanket. Sunlight snuck into the loft behind a nearby blind. He found a note on the nearby coffee table: "Too bad you couldn't stay awake last night. Let yourself out. Maybe next time. Bella."

Marc looked at his watch: seven in the morning. No wonder she took naps after work.

On his way out, he passed the back door of a casket maker. The ajar door showed floor samples resting on sawhorses. He grabbed a cab to his place, changed, and went to his job. His hangover left him wearing sunglasses indoors, hating the noise of typewriters, and washing out his mouth every ten minutes.

Marc called David at his office, but his comrade had phoned in sick again. The secretary still claimed to be unavailable for a date. Marc tried David at home, but only the answering machine took his call. He thought about trying Daphne to see if David had followed through, but decided he would rather hear the play-by-play later from David. He called Bella at home and left a message on her machine asking her to call.

After work, Marc went straight to his apartment and placed an ice pack on his head. The phone rang. He answered as quickly as possible before it drove him insane. "Good evening, this is Bella." Her voice eased his pain.

"Hey," trying to sound lively.

"You called," she said softly.

"I wanted to see you again. The sooner the better."

"I'd love to see you again, but not tonight."

Marc pivoted, "When, then?"

"You tell me."

"How about a ballgame this Saturday?" he suggested.

"What time?" asked Bella.

"It's a day game…"

"I can't make it," Bella said. "But I would like to see you."

"How about a walk in the park?"

"Sounds nice. Saturday evening?"

"Why not in the afternoon?" asked Marc.

"Saturday evening?" Bella repeated.

They settled on where to meet.

Marc lay back and replaced the ice bag over his eyes. He dozed.

Half way through the night, he woke screaming. "What am I doing?" he asked the empty room. He ached from sleeping in the easy chair. He fell on the floor when his legs could not support him. Dizzy, he lay there.

He felt like the smartest person in the world as he realized the truth about Bella. He cringed with horror and trembled at the revelation. He had slept in her loft only the night before.

Marc struggled to his feet, hoping not to vomit. He grabbed a bottle of whiskey, chugged a mouthful, and dropped the bottle as his stomach rebelled.

Rushing to the bathroom, he tripped on the carpet, tumbling head over heels on to the tile before the commode. He bent over the seat, worshipping at the porcelain edifice. After his stomach emptied, Marc leaned against the wall and fell asleep.

The smell woke him the next morning. Through sheer willpower, he flushed the toilet before he threw up again. He cleaned and patched various bumps and scrapes and went to work.

Calling David, Marc learned his friend remained sick. David's secretary still would not go out with Marc.

He reached David's machine again. This time he left a message: "David, pal, this is Marc. I need to talk to you. Call me as soon as you can. It's about Bella. She has something wrong with her. She might be a vampire. Don't fast forward! I'm serious. Think about it, Dave. She only comes out at night. She went for your neck as soon as she could. She drinks Bloody Marys and Marias like they're going out of style. She is very weird.

"Anyway, call me right away. I'm supposed to see her again in two days... in the evening, after sunset. I'm taking tomorrow off work. I need to learn about vampires. I'll talk to you soon."

Before Marc hung up, he asked if David wanted in on their weekly coke purchase or not.

After work, Marc met his dealer and then went home. He crashed early. He had a big day ahead at the library.

Marc arrived bright and early. The library proved to be great for scoping out women. The staff made him feel awkward when he asked for vampire stuff, but they gave him all they had. He tried to persuade the cuter librarian to have lunch with him, but it went nowhere.

Marc read about Vlad the Impaler and he read fiction about New Orleans vampires. He found a children's version of Dracula. Everyone disagreed about the definition of a vampire and what they could do and to whom they did it. Marc decided to prepare for anything on his date.

He went to a hardware store, a market, and a religious bookstore to shop, putting all his supplies in a gym bag.

Grabbing a cab home, Marc had the driver go by Bella's on the way because he wanted to see it in the daylight. A big sign out front announced, "Haberman's Caskets." She must have intentionally brought him in the side door.

Marc decided not to go out, even for a Friday night. He stayed home and watched the tube, another one of those horror flicks with Peter what's-his-name, which proved almost as informative as his day at the library.

Marc woke up around noon and ate breakfast. He lounged around, reading the paper, and watching the Red Sox on TV. He tried David again, but the man would not pick up.

As the evening approached, Marc started on the coke. The shadows grew longer on the floor and moved more and more rapidly. His mind rushed in a hundred directions. He saw Bella kissing him. Her lips pressed on his. She traced a line down his cheek onto his neck, nipping lightly. Their breathing grew deep and furious. Her lips pulled back, exposing fangs to the air. They ripped into his throat. Stars washed over him.

Coming to himself and running late, Marc polished off David's share of the powder. Disheveled but ready for Bella, he left for the ballpark, carrying his gym bag full of tools.

Bella waited on a bench. Marc sat next to her and placed the bag between them. She moved to kiss him, but he backed away. She frowned. He had her then. They exchanged pleasantries.

"What's in the bag?" she asked.

"Stuff," Marc answered, playing it cool.

"Just come from the gym?" Bella asked.

"Yeah, yeah," he said.

They walked quietly for a few minutes.

"What's the smell?" Bella asked.

"Maybe my socks?" Marc tried.

"Do you have garlic in there?"

Marc changed the subject. "What say we go back to your place?"

They stopped walking. She looked at him intensely for a few moments. "All right. Then you can put your bag down far away. Maybe I can persuade you to kiss me in private."

Marc understood it all. She wanted him alone. They would kiss and then she would put the bite on him. Forewarned is forearmed.

They grabbed a cab to her place. Once inside, she led Marc to the sofa. She tried to take the bag from him, but he would not let go. They tugged until he opened it with his free hand.

Bella grimaced from the smell. Marc pulled out the garlic. She knocked it out of his hands.

Bella said, "I'm allergic."

Marc told her, "I believe you."

Confused, Bella let go of the bag.

Marc pulled a large plastic cross out of the bag.

She took a step back. "What's going on, Marc?"

He moved toward her, brandishing the crucifix like a knife.

Bella put more space between them.

"The truth is," Marc announced, "you're a vampire."

"You're out of your mind." Bella tilted her head, as if it might place him in better focus. "Wait, that sounded more harsh than I intended."

"Why don't you own any mirrors?"

"It's a loft. Wait- there is one in the bathroom." Bella tripped and fell backwards.

Marc pounced on her and shoved the cross in her face.

Bella screamed as he grabbed her arms. She kicked him in the balls.

Marc groaned and fell over.

She scrambled to her feet and ran into the distant terrain of the loft.

Marc crawled to the sofa and took a stake and hammer from his bag. Lurching in the direction he thought she had disappeared, he staggered uncertainly. He turned at a sound. Bella hid in the bathroom.

Marc held the hammer and stake like a cross and tried really hard to believe in God which he had read might be a requirement for the crucifix to fend off the undead. He charged into the bathroom.

Bella stood in the tub behind the door, holding a glass bottle. She hit him in the back of the head and Marc crumbled to the ground, covered with shampoo.

Barely conscious, Marc would always remember Bella pulling him up by the hair. She put her hands on either side of his head and kissed him on the lips. Bella slowly moved down the side of his face. Every follicle on his skin rose to the occasion. He must be doomed. She reached his neck and bit.

Marc screamed as loud as he could. Marc screamed from the bottom of his heart. He screamed to God to save him.

Bella stopped. She twisted his head so he faced the sink and pulled him upright. "You're a moron," she said as he stared at the mirror and saw their reflections.

Bella let go of his hair. He fell backwards and his head hit the tub.

***

When Marc woke, he sat in front of his apartment building with a note pinned to his chest. The cross hung from his neck. The garlic bulged in his pocket. The note said "Fearless Vampire Killer" in large print. He pulled it off.

Mrs. Ferguson, who lived below Marc, approached. She led her Shih Tzu by its leash. After tsk-ing at Marc, she mounted the stairs to the building entrance, but her dog held her back while it peed on Marc's leg.

Marc and the old woman watched in silence. Mrs. Ferguson held the door open while he gathered his things and went inside.

The light blinked on his answering machine. "This is David. Maybe you've been hitting the stuff a little too hard lately. You ought to go on the wagon for a while. I can take whatever you have left off your hands.

"I took you up on your offer about Daphne. We returned from the Cape this morning. Get this- we're engaged. I could really use your advice about how to break it off with Bella."

ON THE BEACH

Marinated in lotion and slow cooked by the sun

Singeing at lightspeed all afternoon

Neap, neither high nor low

Accompanied by a lone albatross

The beak devours a hermit crab

While the sand absorbs the chaise lounge

And I sink and I sink and sink

As those black orbs observe

GROSS OUT '23

I was on the phone with my daughter Dora. She needed money for rent because her last audition sure thing hadn't panned out.

My agent, Horton, called after I got off the phone with her. Before I could ask if he could do anything for Dora, he demanded, "You still got that samurai sword? You gotta get over here. I'm at home."

The sword had been a gift from Takeshi Kitano for work I did on a rewrite of Jersey Boys reset in Osaka. I was in the midst of a dry spell, so I did what my agent wanted. Up in the Hollywood Hills, Horton buzzed me through the gate and the front door. Walking into his strangely empty mansion, I found Horton in the movie room.

"What are you staring at?" He yelled.

"Horton, you're a giant penis!"

"I know what I am, jackass, but what are you?" he retorted.

About fifteen feet long and six feet in diameter, Horton lay atop a giant pile of head shots and contracts. "You're a giant dragon dingus, a big chubby! When did this happen?"

"According to my wife, soon as I made partner at the agency." His voice came from the opening in the foreskin. "That reminds me— Siri, call Cuckold, Shield & Wadd!"

While we waited for his divorce attorney to come on the line, Horton said, "Make yourself useful and change the towels under my balls."

I hadn't seen his sack back by the wall. Up close, it turned the air steamy and reeked of wet Doritos. Someone had placed a rack of clean white towels nearby. I used a broom to lever the soaked, yellow brown towels from beneath his testicles, which shifted like roadkill in a burlap bag.

"Richard," roared Horton into the phone, "She abandoned the marital home. I have a right to see my son! He should respect me now if ever! Just do it, Wadd!" He cut off the call.

As Horton shifted on his mound of acquisitions, papers stuck to his undercarriage. I recognized so many faces of actors. They looked so bright and hopeful. "Hey Horton, what's a picture of Dora doing under your left nut?"

"You remember- I got her that role as a barista in that Joss Whedon comeback picture, Bluebeard Takes Manhattan. She got a leg up because of me."

I used my sword to poke through more of the head shots, so many, so young.

"What am I doing here, Horton?"

"Isn't it obvious?" The tip of his foreskin vibrated like a banjo string. A little juice leaked from the opening. "My parents circumcised me as a child and then this transformation happened! I'm trapped in the world's stinkiest turtleneck! When I inhale, I smell old yogurt and armpits!"

Happy to help, I took my job seriously. I used up two tiny tubes of topical ointment from Horton's medicine cabinet before the first cut. I treasured my sword, but it was just a dull replica. It went into the edge of Horton's foreskin like a butter knife into a steak. Horton let loose with something like the sound of a basketball run over by a Range Rover crossed with a metal rake dragged across a blackboard. As his blood drenched the blade, I struggled to saw a straight line. I ran out of towels in the first five minutes. Horton's initial scream became a moan and then silence.

Even hearing about smegma left me unprepared for the yellow green yeast revealed as the ring of skin fell away from Horton's tip. I was unable to reach the skin between Horton and the ground. Besides, the sword had grown duller, and crud encrusted.

I waited for Horton to come around. He groaned. I grabbed the loose skin ring with both hands and ripped it free. All the glass in the room shattered with Horton's scream. I took the skin lifesaver over to the wall and hung it with my sword as high as I could reach. Before I left, I asked Siri to call for a freelance welder. Horton needed serious cauterizing.

DEAD ENDS NOW

"Fucking awesome!" yelled Peter as they stepped out of the blind and approached the dead buffalo.

Eight months ago, Madison Skant might have agreed, but she had never accompanied Peter on one of his safaris. Now the hunts had come to their land in Montana. She had watched while her in-laws marched their way through the last surviving members of four dozen species.

For the longest time, Madison's biggest regret had to be marrying his stupid last name. Otherwise, she appreciated the godforsaken fortune which defied anything being scant in her life. If she wished for it, the Peter provided. Specifically, the family largesse opened its great maw and bestowed.

Peter proved not to be the crack shot he had claimed in his tales brought back from Africa. The sound of the huge beast grunting and thrashing in agony hurt Madison's ears even more than the stench of crap, sweat, and blood stung her nose.

Peter fired into the huge head and then again when he failed to kill the buffalo. Steam rose from its orifices in an admission of nothing left to offer this world.

She placed her hand on her husband's arm. "Are we sure this will work?"

"I've spoken to my parents. You've spoken to them," Peter had stopped using the look which showed he still enjoyed her questions. Instead, he offered the anger of someone laying the groundwork for a difficult goodbye. "It will be fine," he reassured through straight lips. "We don't have time for another conversation."

"I'm not ready," said Madison. "Besides, you pulled the trigger."

Peter's jaw sealed shut as his face muscles tightened. "I expected as much." Never taking his eyes off her, he removed his hunting clothes, revealing his departure bodysuit underneath. "I couldn't wait all day for you to fire."

Two young men wheeled a laden gurney out from behind a tree stand. They belonged to the laboratory which had taken over the large greenhouse. Their first task required the insertion of the armature into the dead buffalo while preserving as much of the animal as possible between metal and outer skin.

Madison watched as they hung the animal tail down and inserted a metal rod into the mouth. Stepping back, they used a mobile app to direct the rod's expansion, distending and disarticulating the buffalo. The sound of cracking bone melded with the squelching of twisted organs into unnatural shapes. Fluids leaked onto the growing dung mound below the animal.

The support structure extended as the workers managed to shift the buffalo parallel to the ground and gently lower it onto a tarp. The presentation looked like a horrifying offering at a wholesale fish market, something for the connoisseurs.

Peter touched Madison's elbow. "We haven't kissed since all this began."

Madison could not turn away from the malformed creature, locked in an unending scream. "You're right. We haven't." She heard her husband step away.

When Peter moved into view beside the buffalo, the body-suit left nothing exposed. Between the goggles and the stripes, he looked like a giant rubber insect. Against his chest, latex covered the most important part of the outfit.

Surgeons had installed cardiac implants with external ports in all the Skants and their chosen companions. When their turn arrived, the Quantum Ethical Device connected to the ports. Powered by a heinous act, the technology transported the wearer to the family's safe harbor on Mars.

That had been the sales pitch. Peter's father had outside consultants confirm the theory and the practice. Those neutral scientists proved that quantum entanglement could replicate a living being a great distance away. The Q.E.D. developers demonstrated their innovation, quantum disentanglement, which granted the distant body independence of action and thought. They insisted they had proven the universe possessed a moral component by using an indefensible act to stimulate particle separation. Q.E.D. admitted this left the problem of two living Peters, one on Earth and one on Mars, as well as duplicates of every other transportee. However, they had a solution for that particular dilemma.

The two young men helped Peter slide inside the buffalo feet first. His arms constrained, Peter could only look at Madison as he disappeared inside the buffalo. One of the men crouched beside the head and pulled the sides of the jaw together. The other sealed Peter inside with a surgical stapler.

Madison had only observed three departures but wondered every time at the lack of ritual. The entire process had become a rote task instead of an ongoing science experiment on live human subjects. Her imagination failed to find appropriate words before it became apparent Peter had left.

The technician with the mobile tapped the screen and Peter's bodysuit released a series of chemicals killing and dissolving its contents. The sides of the buffalo settled inward suddenly even as the area filled with the stench of burnt flesh.

The two men approached the buffalo and righted the gurney, leaving the buffalo hanging tail-down again. The one with the mobile suppressed a nervous giggle.

"Wait," Madison found her voice. Overcoming the funk filling her nostrils, she asked, "Can you open it up?"

They looked terrified.

"We have to obtain permission from Prof. Leererbrook."

"No one's ever asked before."

"I won't tell if you don't," Madison offered her downhill skiing podium smile.

They shrugged. Then, they spent a long time prying and ripping out the staples. Gurgles and gas erupted from the buffalo's interior in a palpable haze. The aperture revealed a devastated interior. Visible burns coated the inside of the cadaver. Peter had departed.

"I think he knew you weren't ready," said Clive, stepping forward to pick up Peter's rifle. "No reason to waste a buffalo on somebody your size. He's the chunkiest Skant so something so large proved more appropriate for him. A medium-sized dog will do for you, Ms. Skant."

Clive had managed the grounds from long before Madison's arrival. In the last months, his entire duty evolved into sending Skants on their way. He had one adult left and he studied her. "I have a river otter on the way."

The family patriarch had dubbed the effort Operation Outlet and converted the grounds-keeping office to operations central. In the early days of the crisis, before wildlife NGOs understood their maneuvers, the Skant fortune donated massive amounts to support RFID tracking of all species large enough to fit a person.

Immediate extinction threatened few animals, so they had facilitated it. Knowing when and where all the members lived proved incredibly helpful. Additionally, farming out last-of-the-line animals to other one-percenters proved lucrative. The cost of sending ahead to Mars adequate building and farming supplies kept rising as the world's humans became increasingly aware of their undeniable end.

Stories decrying ongoing environmental devastation filled her news feed. Accusations of mismanagement by parks and charities and government entities flew back and forth. Representatives of each agreed the recent rapid die-off meant something more ominous than climate collapse stalked the environment.

Normally, three days passed before transported humans recovered enough to talk over the laser bands. Madison spent the interval tracking international news.

On the second day, she walked through the mansion feeling the eyes of the staff upon her. Whatever the general population of the world heard from public media, these people knew their employers had deserted the planet. Whispers of occult happenings in this Montana retreat and other billionaire enclaves had made the gossip news. Clive had been by after breakfast to report he had chased away more paparazzi at sunrise. Last night, Madison had ordered Peter's publicist to deflect all requests for interviews.

"Ma'am," announced Clive. He found Madison standing beside the koi pond. Walking up beside her, he said, "They make beautiful colors."

"Aren't you going to tell me they're pointless? Peter would say so." She stretched her arms out to encompass their surroundings. "I didn't want any of this. I thought it would last forever; be here long after I'm gone. Peter's father bought it and made it into an outdoorsman's paradise."

"None of the family spent much time here until the last few months," said Clive.

"I talked Peter's father into letting me do this. I wanted something I could point to and say I added the pond."

"Such a lovely feature," said Clive.

"You can't see it, but I had them install a PolyTech 30000 water filter and a HighFlow 30000 water pump. We have UVC lights, air boxes, bird scares, thermometers, and heaters."

"You know your stuff," said Clive.

"I do," said Madison, "and none of it matters anymore. When the fish are gone, who gives a shit about filtration and oxygenation?"

"No one, I imagine." Clive joined Madison in contemplation of the futility of koi ponds.

Madison broke the silence, "Am I really the last one to go?"

"Except for the children," said Clive. "I've been in contact with the other Earth-side managers at Sun Valley, Laucala, Bohemian Grove, as well as the New Zealand and Hawaii archipelagos."

"Right," Madison said and then shook herself out of her funk. "What are you talking about? I thought we only had left those too young to know the difference between right and wrong."

"Mr. Skant wanted us to try. He never gave up on bringing all his grandchildren. He set up a program in the farmworkers' former community."

"Show me."

In Clive's Range Rover, Madison said, "I understood we only had a skeleton crew."

"It's true. With my encouragement, the old man dismissed the farmworkers," said Clive, "but Mr. Skant wanted to isolate the children to enhance the possibility of bringing out their... darker natures."

Thinking about a few of the little Skants, Madison said, "I would think the necessary behavior would come naturally to some."

"Unfortunately, those children with an inborn inclination for harming animals aren't able to recognize their actions are morally reprehensible."

Madison nodded, "The reason Curtis Skant has been unable to transport?"

"Exactly. Even with hypnosis and medication, we await a breakthrough," said Clive.

Madison sighed. "So, I'm not the only holdout."

"I understand Curtis remains quite enthusiastic about departing."

"Whereas I'm merely procrastinating." Madison watched the cinder block buildings surround them as they entered the workers' former compound. "What happens to the children who can't be prepared for transport, the ones who are too unnaturally inclined?"

"Same as always. They're sent off to boarding schools in New England." Clive parked the Range Rover and led Madison inside the schoolhouse.

Inside the door, the din from the first classroom made Madison stop in her tracks. A handful of children sat on bean bags facing screens and playing first person shooters against one another.

"Couldn't they wear headsets?" asked Madison.

Instead of answering, Clive pulled the door shut and directed her down the hall.

"Not all those children are Skants," said Madison.

"I can assure you we're following instructions," said Clive. "If I had to guess, I'd say Mr. Skant didn't want to put all his eggs in one basket or have all his eggs come from one basket, if you know what I mean."

"I do." Madison stopped at the next classroom to see the movie which the students watched. "It's a bunch of cut scenes of people fighting animals."

"The child psychologists produced that slop in a hurry. Not their best work." Clive kept going through double doors. "The important work happens in the gym."

"All these kids look the same age, like ten to twelve or so." asked Madison.

"Good catch," said Clive. "Younger and we can't help them. Plus, the ones right past the cusp of puberty are too whack-a-doodle to work with. We treated older teens like adults for the purposes of transport and sent a number on their way."

They heard the gunfire before Clive opened the gym doors. "This is where the magic happens." Clive grabbed two ear protection sets and handed one to Madison.

They stood behind the four shooters. Only one fired her weapon. The young girl wore an oversized eye guard which looked irrelevant to her effort at emptying her handgun as quickly as possible. When the clicking started, she tossed the weapon onto the floor in her lane and collapsed cross-legged and pouting.

At the other end of the children, Madison saw a familiar face. "Tara?"

While many of her niece and nephew in-laws tolerated Madison, Tara sought out her aunt at the first family Christmas when Madison counted as merely another of Peter's girl-friends. The little girl asked if Madison knew how to play chess and glowed after the affirmative reply. After her third loss, Madison had to explain she truly tried. Tara nodded, "I know." The next day, Tara solemnly presented Madison with three books on chess strategy from her personal library. "These are a loan. I expect them back."

Madison embraced Tara. Tara patted her aunt on the back.

"Are you okay?" asked Madison.

Clive came up beside them, "Certainly looks like it. She's close to a perfect shot."

Tara picked at raw skin between her knuckles. "I want to go to mummy and daddy."

Madison's stomach turned as she pictured Tara sliding feet first into a Great Dane. A lab assistant steps forward and sews the body-suited girl inside—then the loud insect hitting a bug zapper sound right before the dog contracts.

"I'm scheduled for tomorrow, 9 a.m.," said Tara looking from Madison to Clive for confirmation.

"You're right," agreed Clive.

Tara looked at Madison, "Will you come with me?"

The next morning, Tara stopped by Madison's bedroom and admonished her to wear her transport suit.

Too soon, the three of them stood behind the hunting blind on the bluff watching the lab assistants lead a Cane Corso out ten yards away.

Tara turned to Clive and asked, "I've been wondering—he's only the last of a breed, right? Not a species. So, it will still work?"

"The device contains the magic, Tara," answered Clive. "All you have to do is concentrate on the fact this is the last Cane Corso in the world. You are wiping them from the planet."

"From the universe," sniffled Tara. She wiped her nose on her sleeve before triple-checking her rifle.

"Are you sure you want to do this?" asked Madison.

Tara nodded, "I don't want to die like Curtis." She pointed at Clive, standing behind Madison.

Madison rounded on Clive, "What's she talking about?"

Clive handed Madison her rifle. "I brought this along in case. The assistants have provided two gurneys." He had leaned a shotgun against a nearby tree.

Madison saw a Bull Mastiff had joined the first dog. She raised the rifle and sighted the head of the big dog. She traced its body to its heart before lowering the weapon. "I can't do it."

"You're doing them a favor," said Clive. "They're dead ends now."

"They're obsolete when you consider what's coming," emphasized Tara.

Afterwards, as Clive and Madison drove back to the mansion, she received a summons to the Operations Center. Peter had called.

Before she stepped from his truck, Clive asked, "Do you remember when the oligarchs started building bunkers all over the world?"

She adjusted the rear view mirror to study her reflection before walking into the OC. "The Russian oligarchs? Not really."

Clive shook his head. "Not just Russian. We had so many billionaires. It didn't take a lot of math to figure out the world could support either a few billion regular folks or a couple thousand super-rich resource-exhausting mirror gazers."

Madison ran her fingers over the dashboard. "Peter's dad always talked around things. I hated it about him. You're not going to convince me all this is a hoax."

"I'm not," answered Clive, "because it isn't. The tech works. But they're never coming back."

"Obviously," agreed Madison. "They don't have any animals to slaughter."

"Any rotten act would do, as I understand it, but this truly appeals to their despicable natures." Clive shook his head. "They did not check the science, but they're not actually whiz kids despite their inflated regard for themselves. Fortunately, they did accept the studies which showed how our current path was not sustainable,"

Madison stepped out of the truck. "Where do I belong?" She did not wait for a response.

With only Madison and a smattering of children left to transport, most workspaces in the Operations Center sat dormant. Concerns about outbound shipments to Mars dominated current communications. NASA and its corporate partners had made a large profit in the last year.

An employee, badge name Ashley, led Madison to the private uplink room. "Thank you," said Madison, promising to remember the face and name, since few loyal retainers remained.

Because of the time delay, Peter's message played first and then Madison responded. Unless one of them decided to rush a second message, their dialog played like an argument masquerading as soliloquys.

"I'm here, Madison! Mostly over the headache and I'm feeling like myself." The accompanying video showed the same Peter she had grown apart from over the last six months. "After my revival, when you hadn't arrived yet, I didn't know what to think. I had them confirm nothing had happened in transit even before I could leave the crèche. Imagine my surprise when they said you hadn't even tried. What's going on, Maddie? I can't do this on my own."

In the five minutes Madison spent gathering her thoughts, another message arrived from Peter, but she ignored it. She hit the record button.

"It's over, Peter. We're finished. You had to know. Your father designed a playground up there for all his favorite people, which doesn't usually include me. He might be right to act his way. No different from the Garden of Eden, right? Animals doing their thing, I guess."

She pressed send.

Peter replied quickly: "You belong here, Maddie. I picked you, not my dad, not anyone else. Me, because you and I belong together."

Madison stewed without replying and left the uplink nook. She found Clive seated in the anteroom. He held a shotgun across his lap. He waited while she sat and stopped shaking. "I take it he didn't convince you to join him?"

Madison took her time answering. "How long do you imagine we have here on Earth, Clive?"

"I hear they've sent the special ones on to Mars from everywhere except Bohemian Grove, but they're planning to execute the three hold-outs there."

Madison nodded. "And up there? How long do they have?"

"I give them two years until the last one dies. They're shit at resource management." Clive observed Madison, giving her a few minutes to get her shaking under control. "Want to take a last walk around the koi pond?"

THAT'S WHAT I DID

I built the pond in the backyard
Hoping to attract bluebirds
But only drew regrets

I planted seeds in the garden
Hoping to nurture pumpkins
But raised a row of disappointments

I built a wall
Of kiln-fired bricks
Because that's what I thought you did

Look in wonder at
My pond
My garden
My wall
I made them all

THE URACHUS AND THE MAGIC CHIN

Lloyd reached deep into the dish pile, his fingers scuttling along the unseen surface of the sink like a crab at the bottom of the ocean. He extracted his son's favorite drinking cup, the one shaped like the head of a dinosaur- Pteranodon, to be exact. Anatomically, the molded cup appeared correct to Lloyd and he should know. His years at the museum, preceded by the doctorate degree, had filled him with a limitless store of Dinosauria. Lloyd knew his winged reptiles. To his dismay, he was not privy to any recent paleontological findings. Perhaps the cup did not mesh with the latest conclusions of those currently paid to excavate and to classify.

"Help! Help, please!" Jess called from the family room. It was a call for assistance, not of pain. Lloyd strolled into the room. His son struggled with his Play-Doh factory. The toddler looked to his father like the exhausted factory worker looks to his supervisor. Jess banged on the lever of the toy to demonstrate his effort. "Help, please?"

"Let me show you," responded Lloyd. Sitting beside his son, inhaling the peculiar scent of the edible clay, he showed the boy the easiest way to extrude the colored mush through the apparatus. "Do you see?"

Jess nodded emphatically. "Yes, yes." Then he elbowed his father out of the way.

Seeing he was no longer needed, Lloyd returned to the kitchen, tossing a few words of encouragement behind him. Washing the dinosaur cup, Lloyd kept an ear tuned to the family room. When Lloyd returned to his son with the cup half-filled with water, Jess accepted it gratefully.

The boy slurped as much water as he could pour into his mouth, dumping the rest on his shirt. As he slammed the empty cup down on the coffee table, Jess announced the obvious, "I'm all wet."

Lloyd reassured him it would dry.

Examining his shirt as he pulled it away from his chest, Jess considered the idea of air drying and accepted the possibility. He returned to his Play-Doh factory.

Lloyd poked through a pile of magazines on the end table. Ignoring the new medical journals, the old anthropological journals, *Smithsonian*, and *Natural History*, he extracted *Sports Illustrated* from near the top. Settling onto the sofa, Lloyd read an article he had started the day before. With one eye, he watched Jess set aside his toy and cross the room to his bookshelf. The little boy grabbed a *Sesame Street Magazine* and dragged it back across the room. After climbing onto the sofa, Jess settled in beside his father, intently imitating his father's page turning and concentrated facial expression.

***

"Go back to work then," said Cassie, trying to watch television and still look interested in having a conversation with her husband. She'd had a long day in the ICU and just wanted to think about nothing for an hour.

Lloyd looked at the newspaper in his hands. "What about Jess?" His legs extended the length of the sofa, across her lap.

"Daycare," Cassie shrugged because it was easier than using words.

"Not a lot of call for an archaeology degree." Lloyd had taught science to high school students back in Chicago while Cassie went to medical school. Her residency assignment came through on the same day as Jess's first birthday. Cassie had put Youngstown-Goddamn-Ohio on her list as a last chance for a cardiology residency, followed by a long string of family medicine programs.

"How would you know?" She fiddled with the hair on his shin.

Lloyd held up the want ads in response. "I know."

"Youngstown's not an archaeological city."

"Archaeological cities are buried by dirt. They're excavated, not lived in."

Cassie smiled as expected. The commercials blared on the television and she squeezed the mute button on the remote. "Did Jess have a fever tonight?"

"Yea. I gave him Motrin."

"How high?"

"I didn't check," admitted Lloyd. "He was hot enough."

"We have to start keeping track."

Lloyd put down the paper. "I thought everybody'd decided it was a virus."

"Lack of any better explanation." She ran her thumb across the remote, anxious for her show to return. "It probably is a virus."

***

Transfixed with delight, Jess played paddy-cake with his grandfather, yelling out nonsense syllables while the old man chanted the more traditional verses. Inevitably, the rhyme collapsed in a cacophony of slapping hands and slippery tickles. Jess would call out for the tickling to stop as soon as his breath allowed. Then, when his grandfather's hands rested, Jess would demand a new round.

The real reason Youngstown had even made Cassie's list of residency programs was that Lloyd's parents lived in Cleveland, an hour away, close enough to grandparents without being too close. The relationship was not strained, though proximity tended to breed contempt, at least on Lloyd's part.

Suddenly, Jess dropped his hands and raised his nose to capture a desirable aroma. Looking around frantically, he searched out something. "Cupcakes!" The little boy dashed to the kitchen.

Lloyd's father smiled at the receding child. "What are you feeding him? He's getting big."

"The usual stuff: table scraps and what he finds in the yard," replied Lloyd from the sofa.

Lloyd's father had lowered himself to his grandchild's height by sitting on a footstool. Now, he struggled to rise from his perch. Groaning, he forced his hips onto the sofa beside his son. "Every answer doesn't have to be a joke."

Lloyd shrugged heavily.

The father patted his son on the leg. "You, on the other hand, look tired."

"Jess hasn't been sleeping through the night. He's been running a low grade fever for a couple weeks."

"It doesn't show."

"When he gets tired or hungry, it does. The doctor prescribed an antibiotic, but they think it's some virus."

"Kids catch stuff and it's gone before you ever find out what it was."

Lloyd nodded. "It's the things you don't know that bother you."

"How's the job search going?"

"Not well. Nobody's hiring. At least, nobody's hiring for enough money to make it worthwhile-- daycare and all."

"Are you sure you want to go back to work?" asked the old man.

"No. I don't know if I like any of the daycares in Youngstown. It's hard to find a decent teacher."

Lloyd's father shrugged more heavily. "You have to trust somebody with him."

Lloyd considered his options for the way the conversation could go: casual and negligible or deep and meaningful. "The problem is I don't know anyone who's done this before."

His father raised an eyebrow. "What? Raised a kid?"

"I never saw any men doing this when I grew up. I'm not sure what I'm supposed to do."

Silently, the two of them chewed on the conversation's new direction. The air filled with freshly baked cupcakes, distracting both. "You're right," acknowledged Lloyd's father. "That boy is the most important thing right now. Everything you do has to be about him." The ensuing silence disappeared when Lloyd's father reached for the television remote control and turned on a football game. "Let's see if the Ravens can lose another game."

***

Jess cried out for his father, signaling the start of Sunday morning. Not for the first time, Lloyd wished his son could unearth himself from his blankets and straggle into his parents room without assistance. Reaching tentatively for the floor with his feet, Lloyd poured from bed and stumbled into Jess's room. The little boy waited patiently. Father received a smile and a moist hug. Jess needed changed immediately. Lloyd settled the toddler onto his changing pad and removed the wet pajamas. Jess had developed a new bellybutton overnight. "When did you become an innie?" Lloyd asked, knowing no answer was forthcoming. Jess sang him a song about Cookie Monster anyway.

Carrying the active child into their bedroom, Lloyd dropped Jess beside Cassie. Instantly, he encircled his mother. "When did Jess become an innie?"

Opening one eye, Cassie looked at him with dismay. "He's always been an innie."

Lloyd lay back down on the bed and sighed. He doubted his memory had failed regarding the appearance of his son's belly, but it felt possible.

Jess poked him in the side with his feet. "Cowboy?" he whispered. Lloyd smiled and nodded. Jess tossed off the covers and climbed onto his father's knees. Rocking back and forth while hanging onto his father's hands, Jess called for the horse to go faster and faster. The ride continued until Jess tumbled onto his mother. After a brief respite, Jess climbed off the bed and ran to grab some books for reading.

On his way back, he tripped and landed hard on the books. Embarrassed more than hurt, Jess cried loudly. Lloyd picked up the fallen child and carried him back to the bed where Cassie enveloped him. Unable to regain his self-control, Jess continued to wail. Looking to his father he held out his left hand with the index finger extended. Lloyd took the hand and held the finger beneath his chin in a tight clasp. Immediately, Jess breathed easier.

"The magic chin," commented Cassie.

"Magic chin," agreed Jess.

Lloyd rolled his eyes, hoping it would always be so easy.

***

Cassie stumbled into the living room, half asleep from putting Jess down for his nap. Lloyd looked up at her, half blind from deciphering want ads. "Should I simply give up?"

Cassie rubbed her eyes and attempted an answer. Catching the taste of sleep in her mouth, she paused for a drink of water. By the time she returned, Lloyd had turned on the television. She sat down and waited.

"What do you think?" He asked, annoyed.

"I think you should do whatever you want to do."

Lloyd looked for some solid ground from which he could proceed. "What about Jess?"

"We'll figure out a way to cope."

"I like staying home with him."

Cassie patted his leg without saying a word.

"I think I'm good at it."

She nodded.

"I don't really know if I am. I feel like I'm surveying unexplored land here."

Cassie smiled at him and said, "You're a good father."

"Yea, well, what about the money? I'm not doing such an excellent job with that. I should have a job."

"You had one in Chicago. You can get one here," Cassie said.

"McDonald's is hiring."

"You can do better than that."

"You haven't been looking in the want ads. I'm not a nurse and I'm not a mechanic. What kind of job is out there for me?"

Cassie turned off the television. "Then stay home." Her voice stayed even.

"I don't know how."

***

"Something's wrong with Jess's navel," said Cassie on Monday evening. Jess curled over his mother's shoulder, fighting the day's exhaustion.

Desperate for a hopeful nugget within the classified ads, Lloyd did not look up.

"I want to call Dr. Lucas," Cassie announced.

Tossing the want ads aside, Lloyd said, "Their office isn't open." Cassie knew this. The next thing Lloyd heard was her voice on the telephone. Lloyd found himself wondering how serious this could be. Cassie was the physician and she could not wait. Maybe Cassie needed more sleep, and the other doctor would reassure her. Funny-looking bellybuttons did not seem so urgent.

***

From the entry to the emergency room, Lloyd could see a pair of paramedics hovering around an infant strapped to a gurney. The child wore a respirator. Looking off into space, the mother stood between the paramedics.

Lloyd found Cassie and Jess at a check-in station near the entry to the examining rooms. Lloyd sat down and took Jess into his arms. He preferred to answer the questions but found himself speaking softly to Jess. Cassie provided insurance information while Jess fidgeted. The boy showed signs of fading energy.

A security guard staffed the door to the treatment area. "Two visitors per patient," announced the sign over the guard's head. A constant parade of distracted people proved unable to read. The guard intoned an ancient form of security chant: "Two visitors per patient. I'm sorry, ma'am, only two visitors per patient. I have to stop you there - only two visitors per patient." Periodically, the guard pointed at the printed words in order to provide support for his position.

Cassie finished answering the intake questions as a triage nurse approached wearing an oversized white sweater covered with buttons. Many bore the photographs of smiling children. Others featured dancing animals. Jess perked up a bit at the sight of the colorful buttons. Lloyd wondered if she wore the same sweater for the adult patients.

Cassie explained to the nurse's quizzical expression how her son might have an entrapped hernia. Lloyd wondered why his wife never prefaced such comments by explaining she happened to be a physician. The nurse treated Cassie like a mother with an extensive medical library and an over-active imagination. Finally, Lloyd interjected a casual comment about his wife's profession and the nurse let out a sigh of relief.

Jess happily extended his arm to have his blood pressure checked. He screamed and wiggled when the nurse tried to take his temperature with an ear thermometer. Exasperated, the nurse looked to the parents for assistance. Lloyd reached out and took his son's hand in his own. With his finger nestled beneath his father's chin, the boy relaxed long enough for the thermometer to take a reading. Lloyd stared at the corner of the waiting room and wondered what the rest of the people around them must think.

"All right let's go on back," said the nurse.

The children's rooms had been painted with various animal scenes. Most sat empty, for which Lloyd felt grateful. He could not handle the sight of a child in significant trauma. The infant whom Lloyd had seen at the check-in desk rested under an oxygen tent. Its mother sat nearby in a rocking chair, her face turned to the ceiling and her eyes distant.

The nurse pointed to a small room in a corner. She left them alone with the door wide open. A television hung in the corner. Jess had fought off his sleepiness at the sight of all the interesting objects which they had passed. Lloyd set him on a modified crib which took up one wall in the room. Three smiling elephants had been painted behind the crib and Jess walked across the mattress to examine them more closely. Swinging his arm like a trunk, the boy pachyderm-roared.

"He seems to be in pretty good shape," said Lloyd, still unclear on the reason for the trip to the emergency room.

"It could be a hernia. It might need immediate surgery," said Cassie, struggling to sound as if she discussed a recipe for cheesecake. "He has an infection. Something's in there."

Not for the first time did Lloyd long to receive a little more for the money and effort invested in his wife's medical education. "Something's in there" seemed like it could have been obtained for less. "How serious is this?" Lloyd kept his tone light.

"I don't know. It could be profoundly serious."

Cassie had spoken with Jess's doctor, another physician, and between the two of them they had concluded that Jess needed to go to the emergency room. His wife had not acted impulsively. He would really like to complain about wasting his time in the emergency room. Nothing would make him happier. Lloyd practiced frowning at Cassie for a few minutes.

"Hello, hello. I'm Dr. Nabors," announced a young woman who rushed into the room. Recognition crossed her face as she looked at Cassie. "Hi, how're you doing?" She had short dark hair and a small sharp nose.

"Not so good," said Cassie, gesturing toward Jess.

"Do I know you from somewhere?" asked Dr. Nabors.

"I'm a second-year cardiology resident at Northside. We rotate through here."

"That's right. You're Cassie? What brings you in here tonight?" asked Dr. Nabors.

Cassie went through a brief history of Jess' fever. Lloyd chatted with his son about elephants until it came time for his bellybutton examination. Having grown accustomed to his mother's stethoscope, Jess happily raised his shirt when asked. Then, the boy screamed as fingers brushed near his swollen navel. Lloyd leaned over his son and placed Jess' finger underneath his chin. The boy's face struggled from fear through pain to relief.

"That's not a hernia," said the physician. "It's too high up."

Jess winced at every touch.

"Watch it respond there when I press here," said the doctor, making the area below Jess' navel move like a teeter-totter. She backed away from Jess, finishing her examination. "It's a urachal cyst."

It seemed to Lloyd as if every other adult in the room sighed with pleasure. Dr. Nabors even appeared to look at Cassie with blossoming admiration.

Lloyd grunted his ignorance.

"The urachus is a vestigial structure left over from the womb. Your son still has his and it's become infected."

Lloyd nodded his understanding, while inside he thought, "I went to graduate school. This will all make sense later."

***

Arriving home from the emergency room, Lloyd carried his dozing son inside. Carefully, the father maneuvered through the dark house, counting steps, and leaning slowly. He gently lay his son down in the child's bedroom. Untying the boy's shoes, Lloyd slipped them off. After covering Jess with a blanket, he left the room, closing the door behind him.

Standing at the head of the stairs, Lloyd could hear the television come on as Cassie settled down to watch. She would try to clear her mind for sleep. Lloyd turned away from the steps and walked back to their bedroom. Perched on the mattress, he sighed heavily. Relieved they had an answer to Jess' unexplained fever, Lloyd could only worry what the future held. He had asked Cassie and she had mentioned antibiotics and surgery. She knew the important part-- not life threatening. When Cassie had heard the diagnosis, she had felt vindicated and curious.

***

Cassie sat in front of the television wondering if Jess had woken up while Lloyd carried him in from the car. After unlocking the front door for them, she had gathered their belongings out of the car and followed into the house. No sounds drifted down to her ears.

Lloyd may have gone to sleep. That would not surprise her. He had always had an easier time dividing his life into sections. The emotional part did not interfere with the practical part which did not interfere with the sleep part.

Later, when she went to bed, Lloyd lay asleep. Later still, she awoke to find herself alone in their bed. Listening intently in the dark, she determined if Lloyd was in Jess' room or in the bathroom. He always made noise in the bathroom so he probably sat with their son. She waited silently for confirmation, but only heard her son sigh contentedly.

Slipping carefully onto the floor, she walked into the hallway, muffling her steps. Lloyd was not in the child's room. No lights shone downstairs. Cassie walked back into their room. Lloyd had probably gone downstairs. Maybe he could not sleep and went to watch television. She shut her eyes and reached out with her ears. Movement and noise rose from their backyard. The open windows and the summer air helped carry the sounds to her.

She went to the window and looked out. Lloyd perched on the edge of Jess' sandbox. Shadows crossed the lawn and obscured her view.

***

Lloyd dug into the sand with a small yellow shovel, engraved with smiling sea creatures. The larger trucks required significant earth moving in order to submerge them adequately. Having buried Jess' toys, Lloyd proceeded to excavate his son's treasures.

Now, the plastic shovel in Lloyd's hand carefully traced moats around the sand mounds, large and small. With a practiced hand, he uncovered the Matchbox cars, the sand tools, the large trucks, and the dolls. After gently blowing sand dust from each object, he lined them up: by color and by size.

"Lloyd?" Cassie's voice drifted over the lawn. She stood in the shadow of the house, clutching her bathrobe about herself. She waited for a response, but Lloyd only continued with his excavations.

Glancing about for neighborhood eyes, Cassie braved the late night backyard. Her slippers shuffled across the moist grass, sounding like tearing fabric with every step. Standing behind him, Cassie watched Lloyd precisely uncover a toy soldier and place it with the other figures queued along the rim of the sandbox. When she placed her hands on Lloyd's shoulders, the strength seeped out of him and his arms went limp. The yellow plastic shovel settled soundlessly onto the sand. "What is it, Lloyd?"

He shook his head ever so slightly and licked his lips. The words didn't come, so he looked at his hands, curled with exhaustion. "I'm afraid," came out of his mouth unbidden. His voice rasped with sand dust.

Cassie did not move.

Lloyd tried again. "I'm so afraid that I don't matter."

Cassie felt herself sag beneath Lloyd's burden and her hands slid from his shoulders. "Come to bed," she said, turning back to the house.

SALT AND IRON

Salt and iron infuse this dreadful soil.
None responsible will ever visit
This snow-covered land recently aboil.

Seek reasons like avarice, crude oil,
Or yours is mine and tat is tit.
Salt and iron infuse this dreadful soil.

Choose your side, do nothing but see the coil-
Death is details; nothing explicit
In this snow-covered land recently aboil.

Become nothing more than the gargoyle
Overseeing the survivors' deficit.
Salt and iron infuse this dreadful soil.

Subdued by madmen who would embroil
Us in schemes to their benefit

And set this snow-covered land recently aboil.

Plead vain ignorance and make children toil
While we watch and debate and, on our asses, sit.
Salt and iron infuse this dreadful soil,
This snow-covered land recently aboil.

When Pigs Fly

We'll need pig blinds.

Bacon will taste different and occasionally include buckshot.

Geese will be less annoying, in comparison.

No longer a herd, but a flock. Not a sty, but a nest.

Airplane engines will have pig-catchers installed.

Even more people will say "when Hell freezes over."

Politician at the Gym

Naked, the big man comes into the shower
Like Hannibal crossing the Alps
His tail sprays feces across the tiled floor
Nearsighted, he snorts at every sound
His bunker mentality frightens away the hot water
Raising goose bumps on trembling flesh
Later, the soft cracks of a towel-whip echo off the ridged walls

Marxism and Critical Legal Theory: Why Groucho?

The fact that [defendant] dances to a different choreographer should not be a reason to deny him, and inferentially all of us, the basic constitutional right to express our feelings whether they are about the flag, dancing or Groucho Marx.[1]

I. Introduction or "Mr. Marx, the Reader. Reader, Mr. Marx."

---

1. City of Billings v. Laedeke, 805 P.2d 1348, 1354 (Mont. 1991) (showing the pervasive influence of Critical Legal Studies)

For too long, the relationship, so clear to so few, between Marx's perception of the evolution of the law and the perception espoused by the proponents of Critical Legal Studies has remained hidden. (A *nihil cum id* if you will.[2]) The zenith of Critical Legal Studies was reached on the radio show *Flywheel, Shyster, and Flywheel*.[3] It is easy to imagine the young Crits lying in front of their radio, paging through the comics section of their local newspaper and listening to Groucho Marx and his brother, Chico, bringing anarchy to the legal profession. As the future law school professors would drift in and out of sleep, Marx's brand of wisdom would seep into their unconscious minds only to peer out from behind their eyeballs after they became members of the Bar.

This Note will examine the obvious influence of Groucho Marx on Duncan Kennedy[4], Robert Gordon and like-minded individuals as demonstrated by their explications of the extreme legal realism originally put forward by the greater Marx,

---

2. No, it isn't in *Black's*. Yes, you should have taken Latin.

3. NBC radio broadcast 1932-33.

4. *See* Duncan Kennedy, *The Role of Law in Economic Thought: Essays on the Fetishism of Commodities*, 34 Am. U. L. Rev. 939 (1985). Kennedy discusses the "lost" Marx brother at great length here. Julius ("Groucho") was apparently influenced heavily by his elder brother, Karl ("Reddo").

Groucho.[5]

II. Precious Little Critter History

The Crits, as they came to call themselves, or the Critters, as they shall be called in this Note, developed a wholly unorthodox legal philosophy. The kernel of inspiration behind the Critters popped into existence in the 1960's at Yale Law School during a Marx Brothers Film Festival. The cinema was unable to provide the proper screen size. Consequently, the picture bled over onto the walls. Almost as one, students and faculty in attendance realized the narrowness with which they had been approaching the law. Apparently, most of them mulled about on the sidewalk outside the theater complaining about the projectionist, the Socratic method of teaching, the lack of Raisinets or Goobers, and recent Supreme Court decisions, in that order. A few of the more vocal members of the audience proposed a series of gatherings where a solution could be found to these various woes.

At their first meeting in a secret and unknown location in New Haven (3939 Walnut Street #5), this collection of great legal minds debated several proposals for a guru. After ruling out Plato, Jesus Christ, Clarence Darrow, Oliver Wendell Holmes, and Stan Laurel, the Critters agreed on Groucho

---

5. Some have mistakenly relied on Karl, who never once made a film. Moreover, Karl was known to collaborate with people who were not his brothers (ask Fred Engels). For a discussion of Karl's work, *see* Symposium, *Marxism and the Law*, 23 Colum. J. Transnat'l L. 217 (1985).

Marx.[6] Various subsequent gatherings were held at all sorts of people's homes as close to Kennedy's place as possible, since he had no car. It was generally agreed that Kennedy had to be there because he did the best impression of Marx and was the only one who could stand to smoke cigars. The movement gained momentum as they moved their meetings to an open air location in New Haven.

Because of an unfortunate incident involving three skunks, some electrical tape, and a blowtorch, a great deal of attention was being paid to the Critters by the local media, the U.S. Fish and Game Department, and complaining neighbors. The time had come to take their philosophical sideshow on the road. The Critters held their first full-blown conference and bar-b-q in Madison, Wisconsin, in May, 1977, after discovering that a Madison cinema was the only one in the country showing both *A Night at the Opera* and *A Day at the Races*

---

6. The Critters have apparently relinquished Jesus Christ to those who espouse law and economics. The Romans doubtless felt differently about Christ's sense of law and order. *See* Richard Delgado & John Kidwell, *God and Gadamer: Politics and Conflict in the Heavenly Family*, 6 Const. Commentary 7 (1989). Delgado and Kidwell's article was a blasphemy. I hope it is a blast for you. This is just the sort of footnote the editor warned me about. Unfortunately, the editor did not do the same for you.

at a time when everyone was free.[7] (A contract was signed with the cinema guaranteeing a preponderance of Goobers and Raisinets.) As histories of the Critters have suggested, the failure of everyone to agree about Zeppo's contribution to the films (let alone Gummo) led to a break with traditionalist supporters of the movement. Others have reported that, during a presentation prior to its viewing, certain Critters' insistence that *Marx Brothers Go West* was not such a bad movie led to the inability of the older academics, seated in the back rows, to restrain from throwing chewed Goobers at the younger Critters.

The remaining Critters realized that the best way to keep their movement alive was to infiltrate academia. Into the Halls of Legal Education aimlessly wandered the Critters. Soon they could be recognized on the faculty of various law schools by their painted mustaches and foul cigars. Surrounded by

---

7. If you doubt the validity of this version of the founding of the Critters, then see G. Edward White, *From Realism to Critical Legal Studies: A Truncated Intellectual History*, 40 Sw. L.J. 819 (1986) and Are *Lawyers Really Necessary? Barrister Interview With Duncan Kennedy*, 14 *Barrister*, no. 4, p. 10 (Fall 1987).

Holmes,[8] Cardozo,[9] Brandeis,[10] and countless other brilliant legal theoreticians, the Critters held forth their icon, Julius "Groucho" Marx.

The movement attained respectability with the publication of a whole issue of the Stanford Law Review devoted to the Critters.[11] It is unclear what result the publication had on Stanford's reputation. Of course, recognition meant the Critters were right all along and they proceeded to appear in every publication available to them.[12] The response was swift and brutal. Marxists were banned from tenured faculty posts in numbers that made one long for the open-mindedness of

---

8. A known fan of the Three Stooges.

9. Had no sense of humor. *See* Otis Flywheel, *Cardozo's Lack of Humor or Fashion Sense in the Garment Worker's Case* (forthcoming manuscript).

10. Preferred burlesque in its purest form.

11. 36 Stan. L. Rev. 1 (1984). The Critters carefully avoided references to their heathen icon, but Stanford Professor Mark. G. Kelman slipped in a mention on the sly. In a lengthy list of positive statements made by Critters (as opposed to the more common thrashing), Kelman quotes French radical Daniel (Danny) Cohn-Bendit as saying "Je suis Marxiste, espece [sic] Groucho." Mark G. Kelman, *Trashing*, 36 Stan. L. Rev. 293 (1984).

12. *See Men of the Critical Legal Studies Movement*, Playgirl, May 1985, at centerfold.

the 1950's. Tons of "Groucho Marx" masks were burned in the street in front of the University of Chicago Law School which left a grotesque plastic mess that some 1Ls swore resembled Harpo's profile when the sun hit it just right. Splinter groups emerged, most notably the feminist off-shoot, dubbed Dumontians.[13] The Dumontians claimed as their motto: "an association that bans women is not the kind women should want to join."[14] Other groups included purists who felt that railing against the system was a pointless exercise and insisted on total silence.[15]

Yes, the Critical Legal Theorists continued and prospered by developing ever-changing means of infiltrating the legal system. During the dry years, sly references to the "incomparable Groucho"[16] found their way into Critter articles. In one article, a list of "noted legal authors" included "Holmes,

---

13. *See* the cast list from almost any Marx Brothers film.

14. Deborah L. Rhode, *Association and Assimilation*, 81 Nw. U. L. Rev. 106, 107 (1986).

15. Harpists, but you knew that. We won't discuss the extremists who wear funny hats and talk with an unidentifiable accent.

16. Kenneth L. Karst, *Boundaries and Reasons: Freedom of Expression and the Subordination of Groups*, 1990 I. Ill. L. Rev. 95, 140 n.184.

Brandeis, Cardozo, Hand, Jackson, and Groucho Marx."[17] The secret eyebrow wiggle and special walk allowed the Critters to acknowledge each other without creating problems for themselves. They would attend Marx Brothers revivals separately, but sit near each other, laughing softly.

Now, the Critters have been reborn and are out in the open more than ever. Their ideas are taught and discussed in law schools across the country. Frequent showings of Marx Brothers films provide constant inspiration and an unending line of disciples. Currently, Critical Legal Studies is a full-blown movement. Once a slight drizzle, the Critters have become an acceptable part of legal weather just as Marx was accepted by Hollywood once he showed he could make a dollar.

III. Marx's Ideological Content: Legal Rules and Reasoning or A Preponderance of Wisdom

Section III will analyze the movement's debt to Marx by examining those of his contributions which are *sine qua non*. This will be brief.

You may be asking yourself, "Just what do the Critters believe?" Of course you may be asking yourself how you read so far into this Note or why there ain't no sun up in the sky. Some have claimed that the Critters are primarily concerned with the false belief that things are the way they are because that is the way those particular things should be. For example,

---

17. Book Note, *The Lawyer's Guide to Writing Well*, 91 Colum. L. Rev. 1562, 1563 (1991).

Groucho Marx walks into a room because he belongs there, not because any other factor led him to make a choice to be in that room. If you have seen the state room scene in *A Night at the Opera*, then you realize the injustice in all this and you can see why the Critters feel the way they do (cramped and a little seasick).

Others maintain the Critters believe that modern legal reasoning justifies rules for society which make oppressive outcomes appear inevitable, logical, and inherently fair. Basically, if you want to get there from here, society dictates that you take the viaduct. You can't swim and you can't take a bridge and most of all, you can't take a chicken. This has become known as the Why-a-duck syndrome.[18]

Marx was a brilliant legal tactician. He dissected a witness with the care of a pathologist. Maybe you would like to consider Marx's approach to the examination of a witness in a case of high crimes against the state of Fredonia. On the other hand, maybe you would not, but you have read this far.

> Groucho: Chicolini, give me a number from one to ten.
> Witness: Eleven.
> Groucho: Right.
> Witness: Now I ask you one. What is it has a trunk, but no key, weighs 2,000 ponds, and lives in the circus?
> Groucho: That's irrelevant.

---

18. The Coconuts (Paramount 1929) ("Why-a no chicken?")

Witness: An elephant! Hey, that's the answer! There's a whole lot of elephants in the circus.[19]

The clarity and tenaciousness of the questioning is enough to make a trial attorney's heart skip a beat. The Critters have pointed to this very transcription time and time again to show how a few *non sequitur's* can really lighten up the courtroom.

Marx did not limit himself to mere trial work. His work in contracts has remained a model for hundreds of attorneys.

Groucho: "The party of the first part shall be known in this contract as the party of the first part."

Chico: Well, it sounds a little better this time.

Groucho: Well, it grows on you. Would you like to hear it once more?

Chico: Just the first part.

Groucho: What do you mean, the... the party of the first part?

Chico: No, the first part of the party of the first part.

Groucho: All right, it says the, uh, [t]he first part of the party of the first part shall be known in this contract as the first part of the party of the party of the first part shall be known in this contract... Look, why should we quarrel about a thing like this, we'll take it right out, eh?

Chico: Yeah, ha, it's-a too long, anyhow! Now, what do we got left?

---

19. Duck Soup (Paramount 1933)

Groucho: Well, I got about a foot and a half. Now it says, uh, "[t]he party of the second part shall be known in this contract as the party of the second part."

Chico: Well, I don't know about that...

Groucho: Now what's the matter?

Chico: I no like-a the second party, either.

Groucho: Well, you shoulda come to the first party, we didn't get home till around four in the morning. I was blind for three days![20]

Joe Adamson, who should be a Critter, has dissected this remarkable contractual analysis.

Groucho and Chico grow increasingly aware of the contract's inadequacies, until, finally, clause by clause, they reduce it to shreds and tatters like the logic that produced it. They ultimately wipe it off the face of the earth. Chico insists on coming up with aesthetic critiques of the prosaic verbiage ("Hey, look, why can't-a the first part of the second party be the second part of the first party? Then you got something.") It's this idea that you can treat a formal agreement with any kind of individualized response that finally kills the whole deal. If there's one thing you're not supposed to concern yourself about in the reading of a contract, it's whether or not you enjoy the sound of the words. There wouldn't be any

---

20. A Night at the Opera (Metro-Goldwyn-Mayer 1933)

contracts left if people went around worrying about clarity, sensibility, and quality.[21]

Critters may cherish Marx most for his commentaries on the practice of law itself. In a friendly exchange of letters with Attorney Joseph N. Welch, Marx inquired about the operation of Welch's legal office. Here we can see Marx predicting a wide variety of issues which would ultimately be dealt with in the Model Rules of Professional Conduct.

> I was a little frightened when I read the imposing list of lawyers on your letterhead. There are at least forty.... [N]one of the legal documents received at my residence ever had more than four names on it.
>
> How do you all get along at the office? Do you trust each other? Or does each one have a separate safe for his money? Isn't there some danger that you and one of your many partners could both be in a courtroom representing opposing clients, and not be aware of it until you faced each other before the judge? Do you have one community storage room for your briefcases- or does each one sit on his own case?

---

21. Joe Adamson III, <u>Groucho, Harpo, Chico and Sometimes Zeppo: A Celebration of the Marx Brothers</u> 288 (1973). That last sentence should keep corporate attorneys awake nights. If that doesn't work, maybe we could try phoning them around two in the morning.

Some day, if I ever get to Boston, I would like to come in and gaze upon this vast array of legal talent at work- or even at play.[22]

Most of all though, Critters remember the Marx who was concerned with the employment of still-wet-behind-the-ears lawyers as in-house counsel by motion picture studios.

It wouldn't surprise me at all to discover that the heads of your legal department are unaware of this absurd dispute, for I am acquainted with many of them and they are fine fellows with curly black hair, double-breasted suits and a love of their fellow man that out-Saroyans Saroyan. I have a hunch that this attempt to prevent us from using the title ["Casablanca"] is the brainchild of some ferret-faced shyster, serving a brief apprenticeship in your legal department. I know the type well- hot out of law school, hungry for success and too ambitious to follow the natural laws of promotion. This bar sinister probably needled your attorneys, most of whom are fine fellows with curly black hair, double-breasted suits, etc., into attempting to enjoin us.[23]

This quote unerringly predicted Critter concerns with hierarchies in law schools and law firms.

---

22. <u>The Groucho Letters: Letters From and To Groucho Marx</u> 301-02 (1967).

23. *Id*. at 16.

Above all, it was Marx's honesty which is the flame flickering in the hearts of Critters. He clearly felt that the truth was a viable strategy for an attorney, when all else failed.

Groucho: Your honor, I demand a *habeus corpus*.
Judge: A *habeus corpus*?
Groucho: You needn't be embarrassed, judge. I don't know what it means either.[24]

IV. Critters Use of Marx or I Spent a Week on LEXIS One Night

Ultimately, Marx's greatness must be judged by the pervasiveness of his philosophy. The Three Stooges have failed to inspire legal brilliance outside of Oklahoma and they are doomed never to have a journal note of their own. ("Woo! Woo! Woo!" "Oww!") However, Marx's renown has spread beyond mere Critter circles.

Groucho has successfully infiltrated the legal profession as the Critters found gainful employment. Use of his wisdom has proliferated at a rate comparable only to the national debt. To the amazement of all concerned, Marx has found his way into innumerable opinions as can be observed by even the novice

---

24. *Flywheel, Shyster, and Flywheel* (NBC radio broadcast, Feb. 13, 1933).

explorer of LEXIS.[25] Obviously, the Critters have allowed his influence to show through in their work. For example, the Critter cheer clearly displays the Marx touch. "If we are not part of dissolution, we're part of the problem."[26]

Perhaps Marx's greatest contribution bearing appropriate credit is the Groucho Marx theory of language significance which proposes that if the law contains the secret words in

---

25. Marx, himself, wound up in court on a few occasions. Normally, he allowed his attorneys to speak for him. For no reason, other than that I located the case, it is worth noting that Marx was once sued for libel. On his show, *You Bet Your Life*, Marx said, "I once managed a prize-fighter, Canvasback Cohen. I brought him out here, he got knocked out, and I made him walk back to Cleveland." Retired boxer Sam Cohen took offense. The Court held that Cohen was a public figure and Marx could say what he wanted about him., even if he wasn't talking about him. *See* Cohen v. Marx, 94 Cal. App. 2d 704 (Cal. Ct. App. 1949).

26. Aviam Soifer, *Confronting Deep Strictures: Robinson, Rickey, and Racism*, 6 Cardozo L. Rev. 865 (1985). For a premier example of Critter thought, consider reading Anthony D'Amato, The Ultimate Critical Legal Studies Article, *A Fissiparous Analysis*, 37 J. Legal Educ. 369 (1987) (concerning itself with the value of coffee and failure to appreciate secretarial help).

the magic order, then it must mean one particular thing.[27] Basically, the law means what it means because those in the know have learned the code. This has proven invaluable to Critters who have contested parking tickets.

For cases evaluating malpractice, Marx has been invaluable in establishing precedent (or at least *dicta*).

> [W]hen... the [State Medical] Board isolates and accepts a physician's testimony... the Board's reliance on the isolated bit of testimony is reminiscent of nothing so much as the old Groucho Marx program in which Groucho would say to the consultant, "Say the magic word and the duck will come down and you'll win a hundred dollars."[28]

In the arena of torts, Justice Sims offered his version of a Marx Brothers film which would result if plaintiff's argument that hosts should be responsible for their guests' smoking was upheld by his court.

Groucho arranges with Mrs. Dillingham to have the brothers employed as smoker-watchers at her party. At a pre-party meeting where Groucho announces the job, Chico is incredulous that anyone would hire the brothers for this purpose

---

27. Larry Simon, *The Authority of the Constitution and Its Meaning: A Preface to a Theory of Constitutional Interpretation*, 58 S. Cal. L. Rev/ 603, 635, 642 (1985).

28. City of Santa Ana v. Workers' Compensation Appeals Bd., 128 Cal. App. 3d 212, 222 (Cal. Ct. App 1982). Let's just agree this is a corollary of the Groucho Marx theory of language significance.

but Groucho assures him the deal is "legit" because, "Some judge ordered it." At the party, each Marx brother, dressed in a tuxedo, is stationed by a large potted palm. The party dissolves into turmoil when Harpo insists upon tooting his horn at guests whom he believes are smoking recklessly.[29]

When privacy is an issue, the Court relies on Marx's classic rule. "This case arises because plaintiff, to paraphrase Groucho Marx, wouldn't belong to any video club that would have him as a member."[30]

Even civil procedure falls under Marx's broad aegis. "Is Small Claims [Court] to become something akin to the old

---

29. Biles v. Richter, 206 Cal. App. 3d 325, 332 (Cal. Ct. App. 1988). Needless to say, the film was never made. Apparently another fine screen-writer was lost to the judiciary. *See also* New England Petroleum v. Federal Energy Admin., 455 F. Supp. 1280, 1316 n.94 (S.D.N.Y. 1980) (using a Marx Brothers' routine to illustrate a point about national emergency legislation); *see also In re* Universal Money Order, 470 F. Supp. 869 n.5 (S.D.N.Y. 1977) (using the same routine written by the same judge to make a different point).

30. Allen v. National Video, 610 F. Supp. 612, 617 (D.C.N.Y. 1985) (using Groucho Marx to defend Woody Allen)

Groucho Marx show wherein the contestant must say the 'magic words,' in order to reveal their reward?"[31]

A backlash has occurred. "[T]he testimony concerning possession of guns, diamonds, and a 'Groucho Marx' face mask was introduced... indicat[ing] that the State desired to portray the appellant as a felon."[32] Most of the backlash though has come from disenfranchised journal writers. "When I read truly hardcore CLS tracts... I usually conclude... that [the author] is only pulling my chain."[33]

No definitive evidence exists that the Critters' brand of Marxism has swept the chambers of the U.S. Supreme Court.

---

31. Webster v. Farmer, 514 N.Y.S.2d 165 (City Ct. 1987). Uniquely, the Court felt that the change of Small Claims Court into something similar to a television game show was a bad idea. Marx was ahead of his time, predicting the basis for many modern legal decisions (i.e., "magic words"). *See* almost any case trying to interpret the meaning of "rulemaking" and "adjudication" under the Administrative Procedures Act, ch. 5, § 1, 5 U.S.C. § 551 (1988). Alternatively, watch a little courtroom TV.

32. Hines v. State, 646 S.W.2d 469, 471 (Tex. Ct. App. 1982). The Court does not indicate whether the guns, the diamonds, or the "Groucho" mask is more incriminating. This could be interpreted as an insult to gun fanciers and jewelers.

33. Daniel H. Benson, *The You Bet Metaphorical Reconstructuralist School*, 37 J. Legal Educ. 210, 210 (1987).

However, it is believed that Justice Scalia does a wonderful version of *Whatever It Is, I'm Against It* from *Horsefeathers*.[34]

V. In Summary

You take legal thought where you find it.[35]

---

34. You and I both wish I had a cite for support.

35. The author winters in Cleveland at Case Western Reserve University, while spending his summers on the rolling hills of Pittsburgh. He gratefully acknowledges the contributions of Ken "Harpo" Brownlie, Suzanne "Sue" Brendze, Jeanne "Jeanne" Brownlie, Professor Kathryn "Louie" Mercer and all the folks down at Pep's Place for Plants, Peat, Plumbing, and All Your Plastic Needs for their assistance in the preparation of this Note.

THE HORIZON IS GINGER AND HELIOTROPE

We could not forego all hope

Though it appeared distant, difficult and plumed.

The horizon became ginger and heliotrope.

Safety appeared as through a microscope.

We felt lost, desperate, doomed,

And feared the end of all hope.

Bearing neither yarn nor rope,

We navigated even as we assumed.

The horizon became ginger and heliotrope.

Advice from the wise and the misanthrope-

Our time was consumed...

We dared not stop thinking about the hope

The wish for tomorrow, the glow of the isotope,
Diffused as through a kaleidoscope...
The horizon became ginger and heliotrope.

The future is feathered and aslope;
'Tis undiscovered and perfumed.
We do not forego all hope.
The horizon has become ginger and heliotrope.

Trigger Warnings

The various poems throughout the book refer to war, bodily fluids, sex, circumcision, existential fear, and politics.

How I Came in Fifth in the 2022 Scares That Care Gross Out Contest: bodily fluids; gross food; fish in body cavities.

To All NW.L.L. Families: mob violence.

Bugs, Nose, Faulkner: serial killer; decomposition; insects.

Gross Out '23: circumcision; genital harm.

Dead Ends Now: murder of animals; frying of flesh; animal abuse.

About The Author

A nail did once go through Craig's foot, though technically it only made a pointy shape in the skin at the top of the foot without bursting forth. It happened near the time he put a screwdriver through his face. Fortunately, it was a Phillips-Head. Otherwise, you could be holding *Screwdriver Face*, which would have been an even thinner book, probably unpublished.

Look for his work in Space and Time Magazine, *Demons and Death Drops*, *No More Resolutions*, *Lovecraftiana*, and *Unspeakable Horrors 3*. He contributes randomly to Uncomfortably Dark.

Visit Craig and sign up for his newsletter at
https://craigbrownlie.com/
Friend him on Facebook. Follow him on Twitter/X
and Instagram. Or talk to him at a convention.

www.ingramcontent.com/pod-product-compliance
Lightning Source LLC
Chambersburg PA
CBHW071130100726

47908CB00008B/2552